SOLUTION 262

SOLUTION 262
LAVAPOLIS

MICHAEL SCHINDHELM

SERIES EDITED BY INGO NIERMANN
STERNBERG PRESS

To Aurore

Preface

This book contemplates an island that does not (yet) exist, and provides some reports on an experimental exchange of ideas related to the question: What is actually possible?

Speculation suggests that everything is possible. But opinions about what is desirable differ greatly and can generate confusion. The world should become more just, freer, safer, more complete, more environmentally conscious, etc. A single opinion may demand what is possible—but when all the opinions come together, their demands are impossible.

The reports assembled here do not form a total picture. They contradict and also agree with each other. Their authors might be enemies in a different world. But once they land on the island, they become part of a social project. Their joint expectation is that society on the island will facilitate ways of living that can constantly be renewed due to this ongoing political, economic, and cultural experiment. This is life *at the same time as the outside world* and its circumstances and changes are not isolated from the influence of its residents.

The following accounts have been collated from interviews relating experiences, insights, and speculations that clearly or latently reflect the present era's discomfort with itself while at the same time nourishing it. The administration of the island calls this a heterotopia, a counter-site, which reveals the real world but also challenges it. The place itself may be unreachable and transient, but it provides the opportunity to detach from the apodictic social or economic reality of the present age—although this can happen in the real world too.

Lavapolis is the report of these instances of detachment.

Dramatis Personae

Alberto, 56, native of the island, director of the Department of Strategic Planning in Faidon Messinis's government

Dasha, 43, resident of the island for five years, Russian-Jewish ancestry, mother of a fourteen-year-old son, works at the immigration department

Diamantis, 103, one of the first settlers on the island, former key figure in setting up the economy under the original prince, Theodore Messinis

Fabio, 48, resident of the island for three years thanks to the Capital Investment Act, Portuguese-Brazilian ancestry, father of three sons, entrepreneur

Faidon, 69, current prince of the island

Friday, 32, illegal island resident, unknown ancestry, member of an activist group

Haruko, 29, unofficial island dweller, Japanese-German ancestry, recent arrival, architect, employee of Goodshare social network

Karen, 34, illegal island resident, from the United States, member of an activist movement

Lazaros, 26, illegal Greek refugee, arrived six weeks ago, unemployed

Padma, 39, resident of the island for many years, Indian ancestry, mother of two sons, Head of Department in the government's Social Fund

Simone, 38, resident of the island for three years, originally from France, poet

Stascha, 41, island resident, recent arrival, Briton of Macedonian ancestry, journalist

Xenia, 71, island native, daughter of a settler family, critic of Prince Faidon

I. The Landing

Simone 1

The cities where we were born no longer exist. The cities where we live, wherever they are, are testimonies to our naïveté and our belief in a better world. They are the laboratories of self-imposed experiments, the stages of our self-conquest. We are the vanguard. Each vanguard has a common fate: it is either guided by a new truth or led astray by a new error. We won't be the ones to learn if the journey will be worthwhile.

Alberto 1

My family belongs to the first generation of immigrants. My Greek grandfather was a mate on the *Attiki*, the ship involved in the first expedition, and later became a citizen with passport number ninety-seven. The other line of my family comes from Tangier and is of Sephardic ancestry. In the early sixties most of them fled to Paris. Rather than staying in Paris, my father accepted a position as a French teacher in the island's newly founded lycée, and one year later married the daughter of my once Greek grandfather.

There are good reasons for feeling a deep sense of gratitude to the House of Messinis, as many of the first immigrants do. In comparison to the social misery and political unrest all around the Mediterranean, the island seems like a safe haven—a very stable safe haven at that. This was not always the case. Our living conditions have their roots in our unusual national history in which two people played a crucial role: Prince Theodore and his son Faidon Messinis.

Just imagine, a World War has just come to an end, your country is on the verge of an abyss and about to descend into another military conflict, and your family—which you're the head of—owns an island that was devastated by a volcano for five hundred years. Now the volcano is dormant. You are technically stateless with a house and a branch office in an insignificant backwater in the Aegean, and you have six old freight barges, each of them around twenty-five years old, which operate under the flag of a country that has just been liberated by the Americans and is completely worn out, both politically and economically.

You approach the island for the first time. It is as large as Malta, situated deeper than any other island in the Mediterranean rift between the coasts of Crete, Sicily, and Libya. Perched on your bark *Attiki*, which is still reasonably seaworthy, you see the dormant mountain, the ribbons of lava, and the endless macchia. In the calm between two autumn storms you launch off and go ashore. Your companion mule brings you to the top of a huge rock, which gives you a view of the whole island. At first you stare in awe. The other end is so far off! Apart from a rocky desert and fields of ash, some still smoldering, there is only prickly green growth. No settlement in sight. The smell of sulphur pierces the air.

There is ample evidence that the island is uninhabited. There are not even any traces of those who once lived here either to sell slaves or be sold themselves. You stare perplexed at the slate-gray plain, which extends out flat to the horizon. Then a mirage appears of a Douglas Globemaster flying toward you at a low altitude. Before you can dismiss this vision, a massive roar spreads over the island. You can see the five-corner star on the tail …

It was in this moment that the man who became Prince Theodore Messinis, later known as "Patron" by the locals, had an idea that he held onto until the end of his life: the island should become a part of America. The distant powerful country would give this island its blessing—from the air, from the water—and he, Theodore Messinis, would turn this blessing into permanent prosperity.

It's very likely that his initial plans were very different from the ones that he finally put into practice. His enthusiasm for America had nothing to do with Las Vegas. Messinis worked at a shipping company and was not a gambler. He was also a republican who as a young man had experienced the short existence of the Icarian Republic. Casinos and tourism were to be the vehicle for attracting American civilization to his island—nothing more.

Pentagon bosses and officials inspected the still deserted coast before the arrival of the croupiers and tourists. Theodore Messinis used political and diplomatic mandates and risky investments as bargaining tools. Probably spurred by a sense of anxiety about any emergence of communism in the Mediterranean, the United States recognized his status as prince once he had granted them far-reaching rights to station military bases there. The Greek civil war was about to devastate the mainland. On one side were the British and on the other side were Tito and Stalin, both sides almost directly facing each other. The island became strategically important for the Americans. The Truman

Doctrine and the military operations that followed on the Greek mainland probably boosted the readiness of the United States to provide Messinis and the island with rapid assistance more effectively than the assertions by the island's lord and master that he would create a workable small state out of this wasteland.

But that is exactly what he managed to do with the help of the very first immigrants—and many of us are proud of this. The patron beat the drum on the mainland in order to attract colonists for his project. Until the mid-fifties, the people who responded were mainly war refugees. After two years, the population had already exceeded one thousand. This unforeseen new half-pint was a thorn in the side of the neighboring states. Foreign investors were not earning money fast enough. The new administration was overstretched by the pace of events. Laws were usually only passed after something had gone wrong—for example, workers dying on a construction site. Foreign journalists disappeared. European countries issued a ban on visits by new island residents. Interpol picked up four-and-a-half kilos of heroin in a cave in Bouno Volcano. Patron Theodore often ended up on the fence, and maybe this position was more comfortable than being at the negotiating table with the American bosses.

The first tourists were GIs and officers who were stationed at sea or in Italy or Germany, and were keen on a Rat Pack revival and a few bouts of delirium. Europe's new bourgeoisie arrived later, followed by the old aristocracy, who promptly introduced dinner jackets. While fishermen set off with their nets and lamps, gamblers moved into the saloons. Everybody got their money's worth—and left behind enough bills to pad the island's pockets.

The patron was accused of having connections with Cosa Nostra. But the files in the state archives do not confirm this. The island may have looked like a copy of Monaco or Liechtenstein at first glance, but with the strong presence of Anglo-American investors.

I share the view of many island residents that there was nothing ridiculous about Theodore Messinis's casino capitalism. In just under thirty years the original prince had helped more than one hundred thousand people to find a new home and turned this home into a place of prosperity, while neighboring Libya fell victim to Islamic fundamentalism, Greece to a military dictatorship, and Italy to political corruption. He exchanged the rocky decks of his freight fleet for the foundation of his principality, which was just as rocky at the outset. The rumors that Bouno had only died down temporarily persisted for a long time. But Messinis was not deterred.

Even in the early seventies, at the height of his success, Patron Theodore apparently suggested to his friends that his vision of a Mediterranean America needed to make way for a new, more radical plan. But he didn't have the energy or the concept. Nobody believed that his son Faidon would be the man to tackle this. At that time he was attending lectures by Michel Foucault at the Collège de France.

Haruko 1

From a distance it looked like a reserve for the 1 percent. It was a high-class beach for people you didn't want anything to do with. Not if you were part of the 99 percent—like me, for instance. Eighteen months ago I tried settling down in Germany again. In Berlin, of course. I couldn't have dreamed that this was only a stopover before landing on a Mediterranean island run by a prince.

My German father lives with his new wife from the former GDR in a Stalinist-style apartment building near Frankfurter Tor. I didn't feel very comfortable around this woman—she was a stranger to me—and after a few weeks I moved to a *manga kissa*, the first that had opened in Friedrichshain, on the lower end of Kreutzigerstraße. In this neighborhood, understandably enough, there are fewer *otakus* or manga freaks than in Tokyo. Most of the visitors are Internet-café refugees and are looking for a cheap place to stay for a short while. But many of them end up staying much longer. The manga kissa on Kreutzigerstraße had not only a wide selection of comics and films, but also good coffee and sleeping capsules that are more comfortable than those in Tokyo's *otaku* neighborhood Akihabara.

Shortly before Christmas the managers at the manga kissa offered me a job. They ran an "@ home maid service." It was my job to organize birthday parties for customers who did not have any friends or family. We were a team of seven people, and we'd host the lonely birthday boys in two rooms at the manga kissa that were decorated with posters of Ichi the Killer and Doraemon the robot cat. The guest told us what he wanted on the program—what he wanted to eat and drink, a cake with or without candles, which music he preferred, whether he liked playing cards—and we'd take care of his physical and emotional well-being. Some would even bring photo albums and we'd politely look through the books with them to create a familial atmosphere.

Once in a while women would celebrate too. One of them, a Swede from Malmo, told me things about the island that aroused my curiosity. She was barely older than me. She cavalierly showed us her forged student ID that got her cheap train tickets. She seemed to have debts at the bank too. This was something I was all too familiar with. Still, she was living down there on this miraculous island in the Mediterranean and seemed to be pretty happy. I wanted to learn more about it. We met the next afternoon at the manga kissa for a cup of tea.

Her name was Lisa and she belonged to a group of so-called social artists who have made it their goal to develop and promote nonmonetary exchange practices. That is, people without any money help each other by lending or exchanging things that they don't need for other things that they need but don't have. For example, someone borrows a color printer from a neighbor and babysits three times a week in return. Services can also be rented. One of Lisa's specialities was writing application letters for people looking for a job or financial assistance from a public body. Her strong points also included brainstorming and ancient Greek.

To my surprise, the group had its legal headquarters on the island. Somebody there had provided them with an office and all the equipment. Goodshare—that was its name—was a nonprofit network with a school that taught techniques of exchange and helped the unemployed to continue developing their professional skills and make these available on exchange-market websites.

Lisa convinced me that these kinds of social activities, if used on a large scale, would rescue the market economy. This is only a paradox if viewed superficially. More and more people are dropping out of traditional social relationships, and the few valuables they own are the things they keep at home or carry around with them—along with themselves. Lisa argued that once the number of those who have no money exceeded a critical mass, there would either be a revolt or consumer society would collapse—or both. Of course she didn't know when this critical mass would be reached. But there have always been lots of people short on money. No one could seriously argue that integrating them into an alternative market system, which runs without any money, was a completely sensible endeavor.

Lisa admired the creativity that people who had fallen through the net were using to try to establish themselves in a new, livable world. The practice of exchanging goods and services beyond monetary capitalism created a new economy where producers and consumers even swapped roles or formed a new class. She also had a name for this: *prosumers*. The deals were based on alternative currencies or online fiduciaries that were developed and spread by Lisa's colleagues with their customers who had fallen into poverty.

The island really seemed to be new ground. Without any home or income, with bank debts of a few thousand euros from student loans, and without any real prospects, it was easy to imagine that I'd be in good company with Lisa and her colleagues and perhaps learn something at the same time.

Fabio 1

We became islanders—and we've never regretted it. This is not a paradise. Betty and I were not looking for a paradise either, but a living space that is worthy of its name: a space to live. Space for the children in school, where nobody is treated as a foreigner, since we are all foreigners. Space for Betty, who set up a language school, where Hungarians and Colombians learn Mandarin together. And space for me too, of course. Living spaces should give you the feeling of being embraced. That is the opposite of the feeling of being locked in. You occupy the space that you have chosen for yourself. That has been precisely my experience on the island, although it is tiny in geographical terms. I have been living in *one place* for the first time in many years, not roaming between them, which for me were often many flight hours apart. This volcanic soil has somehow tied me down, and although I consider myself a fairly rootless person, I am very open to this contact with the ground.

We live in a terraced house in Lavapolis. To be honest, we have never had as little space as here. If our home has a touch of extravagance, it is the view from most rooms that we have of the sea. The colors change by the hour. An upright flat surface that always gently meets the horizon. Just stroll up along it—at some point your fingers touch the sky. Actually, there is a slight curve downward. And beyond is the world of little hope.

Our ties to this new, strange home are perhaps even stronger in terms of time. In a mysterious way, they release us from the past. It sounds bizarre, but the fact that this island was uninhabited for an unimaginably long time in human terms somehow makes it young. Our own new beginning is reinforced by the occupation of virgin territory that we have become a part of. Although the island has been inhabited for seventy years, it does not have any real traces of history, where bygone time is normally caught and stored. This patch of Earth has hardly stored any time.

It seems easier to leave behind difficult memories here. For instance, those of my childhood, growing up in a fraught environment with parents who discovered too late, while abroad, that they could not live with each other. Or my lack of direction during the last few years, which was all the more demeaning the older the boys became and the more obvious it was that we would have to find a stable home for them. One morning here almost three years ago I watched, for probably the first time, two gulls mate in the surf. Suddenly I was a small inquisitive boy on a seaside pier in Espírito Santo. The interesting thing was that it was not a memory. I cannot say with any certainty whether I ever spent any time as a child in Espírito Santo, let alone watching two gulls copulating. Instead of working through a moment in my biography, which has remained a mystery, I simply exchanged my role with a virtual young lad on a different continent. I imagined seeing the two birds with the eyes and heart of the boy. As if I had been the boy in this moment. And as if this fleeting metamorphosis into an unknown child had been evoked by the early, discreet light of that morning.

Friday 1

Apart from myself, most of us come from America and Europe, others from Russia and China. We are a campaign group of artists and web geeks, including Karen, who will introduce her work separately. We found each other on the Internet. At some point a few people decided to come to the island—illegally, of course, and temporarily. Presumably we are now illegal and temporary everywhere.

I was the first to arrive here. It is irrelevant where I come from, but I know my way around the region quite well. As a teenager, I spent some time in Bari. Europe looks like an alien planet from Bari. The Germans or Dutch have long since written off the south of the continent: no productive energy, insane unemployment levels, low educational achievements, corruption, the social premodern. The entire Mediterranean area is a dump for the losers of globalization.

I sometimes spent my summer holidays in this dump. It was a bit strange. Laptops, for example, had not yet found their way to Apulia. People only knew about the Internet from hearsay. Locals would only hang out at the beach on the weekend, in rowdy droves. Many could not even swim. Because hardly anyone spoke English, I had to speak Italian. That was quite an achievement.

When I was a few years older, I would sometimes take the ferry to Patra with friends, and I hitchhiked through Albania and Greece. We even visited the island once. Someone told us about the casinos and the huge airport. I found it all pretty bizarre in comparison to the little snow-white villages on the other islands and the tramps in Bari.

Despite this, the idea had taken root to return at some point and see what had happened to the casinos and the airport.

Having worked in Africa and India for a fairly long time, this idea suddenly occured to me again. We were relaxing on an island off the Tanzanian coast where there was only one hotel. No city or electricity anywhere in the vicinity. At night you had the feeling of being in space. I imagined what the world looks like from above—clusters of light with a few dark spots. The spots were the areas without any civilization. Other people may think that these are the last places where paradise can still be found. But I had seen firsthand what paradise looks like without electricity. Without schools, without any medical care. Then I remembered the island. I had heard that an experiment was taking place there. I imagined the dark Mediterranean with a pinpoint of light in the middle.

A few months later I took a look at it. The Biography Fund in the Agora. The apparently serious attempt to create universal transparency in the public arena. There are good reasons for remaining skeptical and guarding against excessive optimism. Well, perhaps this really is a heterotopia. But can a heterotopia survive? No one knows for sure.

However, it's not worth it to duly agree with the eternal skeptics back home. This pessimism annoyed me and my friends. No one believed in a future anmore.

It was a disease, a plague. You might say we've found protection from this disease on the island. Some commute to the mainland, others have their home on the island. Every now and then we return to the cities that we left for some kind of project. But we mostly operate on the Net.

Simone 2

Four years ago, Jean-Luc received an offer to take over the chair of probability theory at Amari University here on the island. We moved provisionally at the start. The children, Hervé and Nathalie, were in primary school, so we didn't need to lose sleep yet over whether our highly talented youngsters would develop their genius outside the French education system. We could have returned to Paris during the first two years, because they had made Jean-Luc's successor the deputy director at the Poincaré Institute and he was about to retire, leaving the position open. If need be, Jean-Luc would have found something in the provinces. We were no longer interested in Paris anyway.

My slight sense of disdain for French schooling, by the way, was not just about our children, who perhaps really are gifted. No, it was about the arrogance that dominates the tone of our national education system. It is terribly underdeveloped, authoritarian, and self-centered. Its graduates are rarely prepared for today's world. I mean the world where France is just one country among others.

The girls' boarding school where I was raised only accepted children from families who had relatives that were members of the Legion of Honor. Like my paternal grandfather, who fought on the side of the Royal Air Force against the German Luftwaffe and flew in many sorties. The boarding school was located in a former Ursuline convent built in the seventeenth century. Presumably no renovation work had taken place out of a subservient sense of respect for history. There were sixty bunks lined up in our dormitory, one next to the other, as in Napoleon's day. At each end was a toilet, an innovation from the era of the Industrial Revolution. We were not allowed to use hot water in the mornings, even if there was snow outside. There were punishment cells for the slightest offense. The morning began with mass and the other sopranos and I had two performances at the abbey on Sundays. This was how we were prepared to cope with the future at an elite school in the 1980s. And not much has changed at this boarding school in the meantime.

Our provisional arrangment has become a fairly stable new home. Jean-Luc has signed a long-term contract, and we live in a suburb of Lavapolis, one hundred meters from the beach. Hervé and Nathalie have English and French lessons and are also learning Mandarin. Nathalie is a passionate little fencer, while Hervé is one of the youngest junior swimmers on the national team.

Everyday life is not difficult here. The island is managable and public life is well organized. We have everything we need and nonessentials aren't missed. I have much more time for myself here than in Paris. I now have the opportunity to write again for the first time since Hervé's birth. I work for an online magazine that focuses on contemporary literature. The authors live in about forty different countries and report on literature in their homelands. I review new releases in France and on the island. Of course there is no real scene here. But now a few publishers and magazines have sprung up. Most writers and journalists are foreigners who, like me, are trying out the island as their new home.

A few months ago I realized that all the newly available time is only the outward reason for these changes in my life. The island has released something in me, literally. It has given me access to memories that I had managed to suppress for years. Memories of Paul and Isabelle. I lost my first husband and our daughter in December 2004 at a hotel on Patong Beach in Phuket.

Maybe I still need time to understand why it took me so long to consciously think about my life again before Jean-Luc appeared. Jean-Luc is Paul's brother, by the way. Both our families had spent Christmas together. His wife and my nephew Sébastien died in the same tsunami disaster. We were the lucky ones, if you can say that of survivors. He was sitting with me and his daughter Nathalie on the terrace at breakfast time when the second wave struck and caught the others in their rooms unawares.

I think Jean-Luc has a different way of grieving. Sometimes he talks about that time as if it wasn't over yet. The contradiction between physical loss and emotional presence does not seem to be a problem for him. I do not normally tend to draw these kinds of conclusions, but in his case I truly believe that a mathematician's ability to think abstractly helps him to cope with distance and proximity at the same time.

Proximity totally overwhelmed me at the start.
When I had identified Paul and Isabelle in a camp of
tents and the two of them were wrapped in plastic film
before my very eyes, I had the feeling of being wrapped
in plastic myself. Although Jean-Luc told me later that
he was very surprised by my composure, I still do not
know how I managed to travel back to Paris. At some
point I found myself cowering in this strange apartment in the rue de Sévigné, where we had moved four
years earlier, between unfamiliar pieces of furniture
and clothes that we had bought together. I only went
out once a week to buy something to eat. Sometimes
I looked at myself in the mirror. I wore Paul's leather
jacket, which had been found in the pool behind the
hotel a few days after the tsunami.

This was followed by an equally vegetative
stage of life. I went to clubs in Oberkampf every night
and often ended up, coked out of my mind, in bed with
guys I had no desire to become acquainted with.

I had avoided Jean-Luc for a long time. But
six months after the disaster, he came by every day
after work. He often fell asleep on the sofa in the living
room. This new constellation initially had nothing to
do with love. It just stopped me going to the clubs. A
year later, we set off to find an apartment together.

Common sense played a major role on both
sides. We had survived together on that terrace.
Nathalie needed a mother. And I needed a family. After
Hervé's birth, it was suddenly as if Paul and Isabelle had
been erased. It was embarrassing to me at first that I was
unable to precisely remember their faces, but now I had
these other people around me, and that did me good.

I first dreamed of Paul eighteen months ago. I woke up with an unbelievable feeling of bitterness. I realized that the plastic film that had enshrouded me in Phuket had not yet dropped away. It separated me from my previous life with Paul and Isabelle. The dream repeated itself a few times. I was on the beach with Paul. But I could not remember any more after waking up. There was just this bitterness, but it was no longer as strong. As I see it now, the dream helped me to bid farewell to Paul and Isabelle again, despite this unspeakable grief. And accept my new life. And accept the island.

Paul and I had studied philosophy at the Sorbonne during the same semester. It is a well-known fact that people do not study philosophy for reasons of employment. Paul later became a lawyer; I became an editor of cultural-studies books. Our thoughts were dominated by our lives and the specific society that surrounded us, which we believed to be the right one, despite all the criticism. Our thinking was paradoxically positive *because* it was critical. Society in Paris, France, and the West demanded a critical attitude from its citizens, an intellectual willingness to reject it in order to resolve the dialectic contradiction between maintaining power and questioning it in an environment of social harmony.

This kind of thinking seems impossible to me now. The balance between maintaining power and questioning it has been destroyed. There are, however, two Manichaean camps that either want to destroy everything or keep everything intact. Both positions are destructive, indeed deliberately destructive.

So you might say that I stopped thinking a few years ago. I did not want to come to terms with this destruction. At the end of my time in Paris, I was performing my work as an editor like a bartender. I couldn't be bothered about the customer on the other side of the counter or the drink that I was serving.

Today I am trying to think again. But it's not clear if I will succeed or what the consequences will be. The island automatically turns any social certainty on its head. Others accept this, but I have to consider it all.

This contemplation is leading me back to a life that had completely disappeared: life with Paul and Isabelle, life in a country, a city, a society that have been renounced and that I have left behind.

I'll now report on this contemplation.

Stascha 1

Newspaper articles ostensibly spread the truth. Most people may actually believe this. Journalists, however, rarely do. If we have fabricated the report ourselves, we can easily spot the fly in the ointment, and if it's from somebody else, we'll look hard to find it—unless the report is really a shocker. Not because of its truth content, but because it stimulates our imagination.

For example, scientists on the International Space Station recently made an interesting discovery. Eighty percent of the total mass of the universe is known to be untraceable, and for the first time researchers proposed an explanation for why this might be: a large part of this mass is dark matter that we cannot pick up with our telescopes.

This insight may have triggered no more than a short-lived nod of approval in most readers: Great, science is making progress! But I am a journalist. This harmless-sounding item of news from a hardworking American research institute took me on a dangerous journey. This trip led me first through the growing inventory of critical deliberations I'd been harboring for a few months about the state of the world economy, and then to this strange island.

As I read and reread the news about dark matter I considered the fact that cosmic riddles are not that different from those on Earth—from the current secrets of our capital world, for example. Capital, as confirmed by recent offshore leaks, is also dark matter. In fact, space explorers should be envied: at least they know how much mass is missing from the universe to make it complete. Who could ever say with certainty how much money there is in the world? How much of it does global society lack because it is kept hidden by an infinitesimally small fraction of people?

Beset by questions like these, I could see the capital black hole in front of me. A view into the bottomless void. And the hole was growing! I imagined that three times the worldwide gross national product (the current amount of known offshore capital) was perhaps only the tip of an outlandish tidal wave. Our transparent economies suddenly shrank to the size of Samoa and Fiji, surrounded by endless, voracious, gurgling water.

I concluded that this silent ocean of dark matter could easily swallow up our islands. Geography and transparency apparently have a reciprocal relationship to each other: the smaller the territories where the money is hoarded and laundered, the greater the flows of capital. And once again questions tormented my imagination: Are our governments too weak to break the power of the dark matter? Have our intelligence services and investigative journalists resigned in the face of what seems to be the refined inventiveness of offshore engineers? Are we helplessly at the mercy of global financial capitalism?

Eventually I got tired of this perpetual questioning. I was ready to get away from it all. I boarded a plane belonging to an airline that became successful through price dumping and landed in paradise, not 190 nautical miles west of Greek territorial waters. I wanted answers.

So here I am, still a bit shaky on my legs due to the notoriously narrow rows of seats on the plane, still slightly irritated by the glistening sunlight that matches the adverts. But thinking cannot be repressed or corrupted. My critical faculties, which make me who I am, are returning.

I realize that thousands are queuing up in front of soup kitchens over there in Athens and Iráklion. People are holding banners and competing for every available job and children are unable to go to school because they are so hungry. While this is going on, international colonies of high-end tourists wade through the golden sands of Leisure City, kept refreshed by Moët & Chandon and Thai massages, before heading out on a rented yacht for a cruise through the still sun-drenched archipelagos of southern European economic misery or returning for a casual game of baccarat at the hotel's casino.

Those of us who aren't gamblers or don't feel at home in this kind of company stay on the beach to ruminate. My imaginative powers have not yet dried up. Something sticks in my throat and not even a glass of bubbly or mineral water will wash it down.

An image emerges, from the past. Followed by even more images. Beautiful rich people with cigarette holders between their manicured fingers and chinchilla fur around their marble shoulders stand at a roulette table. In front of a cabaret stage. In a beach chair. With a glass of Moët held up to their freshly glistening lips. The good old postwar period of economic-miracle capitalism.

For a moment I'm uncertain. Did I just dream up these images or did I actually, physically see them in front of me on the beach? Weren't these people just sitting around here? It almost seemed as if time had stood still. There has been no sign here of a recession, stock-market crash, currency crisis, or mass poverty.

Despite my usual spontaneity, I naturally prepared myself a bit for this island visit. I read, for example, that they are experimenting with measuring time. The government implemented the absurd notion a few years ago of setting the local clocks back by one minute compared to Greenwich mean time. The world is sent and received here with a delay of one minute.

But this seems to be a deceptive maneuver. The real time lag with world events should be more like seventy years. That is how long ago it was when the now-deceased genitor of the current head of the island made use of the turmoil of the Cold War, which had just started, and exploited a new appetite for short

35

holiday breaks. He imported a hotel together with its grisette shows à la Lido de Paris fresh from Las Vegas and jinxed the island with the cheap magic of lawless gambling dens and ruthless fast-food tourism.

Well, now the Stardust Hotel is closed and may soon be demolished. It still strains upward, proud as always, like the bombastic tinsel of its architecture, still flamboyant if rather rusty. Groves of pine trees separate it from the beach of Leisure City, the supposedly eco-friendly successor, and remind people of the dubious origins of the island's fame and wealth. Wealth in particular reached a height at the end of the fifties, thanks to the profits from the casino, show, and tourism business, which allowed the ruling caste to forgo any tax revenues and transform this beautiful little piece of land into a sleazy center for money launderers and crooks …

The sun is approaching its zenith. A parasol is necessary. I never take guidebooks to the beach and rely solely on my memory once I have entered foreign surroundings. I remember that the island, despite its current pseudo-democratic facade, is an incomprehensible political relic of a feudal past. A small shipowner on Ikaria grabbed something for himself at the end of the Second World War. The commercial, legal, and diplomatic shady tricks that he used to persuade the Americans and Britons about the legality of his ownership of the island in the middle of the Greek Civil War currently elude any public inspection due to privacy laws.

Although just arrived, I'm already one of the presumably respectable crowd of journalists who are looking forward to the publication of the documents from the state archives in 2031. Anticommunism will certainly have played a role. And the mafia. People say that the father of this nation was closely related to Meyer Lansky, the longtime godfather of the American underworld. Is it not strange that the same Meyer Lansky established the first offshore bank in Switzerland in the thirties? This and similar confidential male friendship may have helped the fledgling prince to turn the dead island into the "Las Vegas of the Mediterranean" (*Time*) in little more than a decade. As a result, even traditional casino centers like Monaco fell on hard times for a while.

Meyer Lansky and his local crony, the shipowner, are obviously no longer a force. And the days of the "Las Vegas of the Mediterranean" are also a thing of the past. In the late seventies the economic downturn tampered with the traditional gambling industry, and mounting pressure from Europe led the young heir to the throne to abandon the old business model.

So is the island a "normal state" now? This is basically the question that brought me on my journey here. It's the product of my curiosity, triggered by an innocuous report on dark matter in outer space. If you can believe the most popular article on this island, these people view themselves as members of a model society, setting an example to the bankrupt and corrupt neighbours in Europe and the rest of the world. It is a stable alternative in the stormy ocean of boundless monetary capitalism.

But I am a journalist and seldom believe what I read.

Diamantis 1

I was here from the beginning. Well almost, anyway. Kurios Theodore was standing in the vineyard one afternoon and told me he needed me on this other island. I had been managing his winery for five months back then. We grew Kotsifali grapes, which are almost as large and dark as plums. They had told us a lot about the island at home in Ikaria and that my master would be going there. But we did not have any precise information. The initial fighting, which would lead to this cursed civil war, was just starting in the north. The navy had paid me off six months earlier. All in all, I had spent seven years in military uniform—seven years in which I had lost my parents and my bride.

I did not hesitate for a moment and went with him. We first lived in a hut on the beach, where the tennis courts of Lavapolis are now located. The bay is relatively safe during storms. That is what we thought, at least. In front of the hut, there was a dock where people arrived on a daily basis, most of them refugees from the Greek mainland, mostly in pitiful sloops. I would register them and allocate beds in the barracks on the other side of the dunes.

The hut was washed away along with the dock on two occasions, together with our books. If people talk about illegal immigrants nowadays, I always think back to our registration books. They are lying off the coast with the names and addresses of all who landed there on the island at that time. A few hundred names just hurled into the sea. But we kept the people. Unlike what happens today.

Padma 1

My dear mother gave birth to me in Aluva, Kerala. I have two brothers and two sisters who live quite close to our parents with their families and we respect them very much. I was the only one to move away. Aluva is now a suburb of the capital Cochin. It is very famous in India because of the temple where the halahala poison was stored. The poison had risen from the sea in the form of mist so that neither the Devas nor the Asuras could drink the amrit. Amrit is the nectar of eternal life. The Devas and Asuras died. But then Shiva drank the poison and took it in his mouth to Aluva. This is why we say, if anybody wants to drink amrit, they must first swallow the poison.

Our people truly swallow a lot of poison. And rarely get any nectar.

I do not believe in Shiva, but God has been kind to me. My father was an accountant at the Federal Bank and provided a bank apprenticeship for three of his children. My brother Ajith has now taken over our father's job. I switched to Citi in Ernakulam when I was twenty. The office was right next to the Cochin Stock Exchange. My parents love their children above anything else and made sure that we received a good education. Of course, they were proud of my promotion to Cochin. Three years later when I received the offer from the bank to come to the island, they were rather concerned. Everyone in Kerala knows that it is best for young people to look for their sip of amrit somewhere else. However, they had heard very little about the island back then. They would have preferred to see me in Bombay or the Gulf. But the bank was setting up a new office on the island and I was supposed to be there from the outset.

So I came here. I've never regretted it, although it was not easy. There were only two women in our team. The other one, Lorraine, came from Bombay. She was a few years older and had left her family at home. It was the usual story, a husband who didn't look after anything. Lorraine was still a fun girl and helped me cope with my initial loneliness.

At first I worked sixty hours a week on average. I commuted by bus between the one-room apartment in Lavapolis, which was mainly a building site at the time, and our branch. The people on the bus sat there like me, tired and alone and not knowing a great deal about life on the island. But I still managed to recruit employees and was later head of the financial consulting department and got to know some people that way.

For example, Dimitrios, a real islander. God helped me discover his heart and we got married even before I had celebrated my second anniversary on the island.

At first everything appeared very simple. Dimitrios managed a workshop for sailing boats; the Citi branch gained customers. Ioannis and Shashi were born and grew up in a sheltered environment. When Citi shut the office after the big crash in the USA, I lost my job and the Social Fund supported me for about seven months. I thought about things a great deal at that time. Shashi was feared to have glutaric acidemia. Fortunately it turned out to be not the case. Work at the boatyard had almost ground to a complete halt since the beginning of the crisis. On a few occasions it even looked as if it would devastate the island. The tourists stayed away and the laws of capital, which were responsible for attracting funds, had not yet been passed. I started a continuing-studies program in public administration during those seven months, and also, after completing the standard tests, I became a fully entitled islander.

The period of drinking poison then came to an end. I was offered a job as a project manager at the Social Fund. All of a sudden it was my responsibility to allocate subsidies to needy people and nonprofit organizations.

I haven't overindulged in nectar since then. I am now looking after projects with a financial scope almost equal to that of my time at Citi. But there is a subtle difference: this time it concerns public money that benefits life on the island. Our two sons are studying at Amari University. Ioannis will probably even take over his father's boatyard. Shashi is a nerd. Accordingly, his real life takes place on the Internet, much to my disappointment. Things will certainly change at some point.

When I lost my job at Citi and was rescued by the Social Fund, I started to view the island in a different way. Nobody would have paid any attention in Kerala. My brother, for example, was only able to stay at the Federal Bank because my father took early retirement in order to benefit his son.

It is not big money that is turning this small patch of earth into a promised land. Nevertheless it does attract gifted and ambitious people. That's key. People with whom you can establish something. When I say "gifted," I don't just mean experts and top talents, and certainly not millionaires. Even a cleaning lady and a bricklayer can be gifted or ungifted. Many arrived here empty-handed. They have been not showered with riches, but they have been given a chance. Yes, you have to work hard. But why not? What counts is that we have a labor market that is not closed at the top. You can make your way up the ladder. Even as a cleaning lady or a bricklayer.

And then there is the matter of religion. God alone knows why He created so many different religions among people. In my former home country, God has many names and there is virtually no dispute about which of them is the true God. Things are similar here. People have all sorts of religious backgrounds. Dimitrios was brought up in the Orthodox faith. I was brought up a Syrian Catholic and still practice. We were married in the ecumenical church in Lavapolis. The Sunni mosque, by the way, is just a stone's throw from the Shiite mosque. But nobody throws stones here.

I have heard of people who have rediscovered their faith in God here. People who live there may call Kerala "God's own country," but Dimitrios and I believe that our island really deserves the title.

Alberto 2

Although I grew up in times when the Strip would bathe the southern sky in what seemed to be never-ending twilight every evening, my conception of the island's history has been dominated by the enormous changes that have taken place since Theodore's second son Faidon assumed office in 1981. This may be because

I started to study piano at the Salzburg Mozarteum in 1975. It is true that I had to abandon music after a few years because of focal dystonia, however, I ultimately switched to economics at Oxford. I was twenty-three when I returned home.

The death of Patron Theodore on April 21, 1981, was less of a surprise—because of the abrupt deterioration in his health in the months leading up to it—than the decision about hereditary succession. Leonidas, who is three years older than his brother, had waived his opportunity due to health reasons in a secret agreement with his father, which only came to light after Theodore's death. He has lived for many years off private money as a recluse in Macau.

Faidon, then thirty-five, had been a nominal member of the governing council since his return from Paris in 1976. The council consisted of four executives, but his leadership talents never found expression during that time. His inauguration took place after a usual period of mourning during the summer of '81, and it already spoke of a "diversification of our livelihoods." Any careful observer could immediately recognize that Faidon had big plans and did not intend to simply continue Theodore's policies. His renunciation of court ceremonies in favor of a folk festival also hinted that he preferred a new style in dealing with his subjects.

Some of the changes that would soon take place first seemed to me and many other islanders like a severe break with the past. In reality they had been prepared after 1976 and, according to the documents in the state archives, had been discussed in detail with the father, Theodore. The rewording of the Protectorate Treaty, which the patron had signed in 1948 with the United States and which had been recognized by Turkey in 1962 so that it could join NATO, restricted the previous obligation to consult the Americans on important foreign-policy issues. The minister of state was no longer appointed by the United States—as it had been in the past—but was recommended by the patron and then approved by the US government. Eleven years ago this rule was finally abolished in favor of a straight consultation.

The principality gained independence from the United States in terms of trade and subsequently joined various international organizations like the United Nations. Since 2000 the island has had its own representative office in Brussels. History, of course, is not as straightforward as I am reporting here. But things would have been different if Faidon had not quickly become very popular with the island's residents. I was grateful that fate kept me from becoming a pianist. On my return from London, I was one of the first economists with an international diploma *and* local citizenship. Until then, government business was mainly in the hands of foreign consultants. Faidon had set himself the goal of changing this. He believed the island needed to gradually become independent in administrative terms and replace the international advisers.

As soon as I learned about these ideas, I applied for a job in the chancellery with my precious Oxford diploma in my pocket. Faidon sometimes conducted the interviews himself. That's how he hired me personally. I soon belonged to the work team of a man who was to become very important to me and to the island: Stanislav Martel. Martel was a companion of Faidon from his Collège de France days. As I was to discover later, Faidon and Martel had also studied mathematical statistics and probability theory at the same time. This combination of sociological and stochastic thinking and the scientific ambitions of the two friends led them to write a research paper together in 1984. It forms the basis for the main principles of island politics, which are still in effect today. More about that in a minute.

Martel's mandate was to reform the state ministry. This mainly involved establishing a Department of Strategic Planning. We initially had an office with three employees who were directly answerable to Faidon and had access to him at almost any time. The Department of Strategic Planning, which I have been managing since Martel retired four years ago, now employs 268 people.

It's often been suggested that Martel was a Marxist romantic who, following in the footsteps of Walter Benjamin, tried to relocate an aura of political awareness that had been lost through modern capitalism and its modes of reproduction, and misuse the island as a laboratory for global-conspiracy concepts. These kinds of claims only served to foster diplomatic intrigue or were simply based on ignorance.

Besides, the research paper and its underlying concept of society had two authors. Faidon viewed himself—and still does, justifiably so—as an academic who puts his research interests to use in his role as a statesman. To be absolutely correct, we should call the research paper by Faidon and Martel an essay. Its chains of thought can be traced back to the men reading a text by Foucault, which remained unknown for a long time and only came to light in the public arena in 1984—"Of Other Spaces." The two authors never said anything about this fact, but we can assume that they became aware of the text itself through their lecturer before it was published.

"Of Other Spaces" identified several areas that, in Foucault's view, differ fundamentally from the core values of societal order. Foucault, who wrote this text in Tunis in 1967, not far away in geographical terms, and was possibly influenced by the proximity of the island, referred to these places as heterotopias or counter-sites where "real sites ... are simultaneously represented, contested, and inverted."

Faidon and Martel's essay has consequently been called a manifesto for a political heterotopia. However, the authors deviated from the considerations of their teacher Foucault in one important respect. He had primarily included cemeteries, theaters, or libraries as heterotopias—that is, spaces whose purpose has already been determined and, in this purpose, persist as an irresolvable antithesis to the interior of society. Faidon and Martel refused the apodictic stasis of this approach. Foucault's "other spaces" were condemned to be different forever. In order to overcome this stasis, they developed the concept of a dynamic heterotopia that not only represents and questions the world, but also that can change its position and therefore be far ahead of the rest of the world. Faidon and Martel concluded that the island was exactly this kind of counter-site, in the sense that it has the potential to reflect, and be one step ahead of, the inner world of the international community and its regulations.

During the last thirty years we have primarily been concentrating on interpreting this research paper and implementing it in our society. This did not occur without some conflict. For instance, we managed to reduce the US military presence to a small outpost on the southwest tip of the island. The current constitution, in addition to addressing general human rights, is based on four reliable strategic pillars: populist democracy, universal solidarity, neutrality in foreign policy, and the Autonomous Territories Cooperation.

Karen 1

Hi, I'm Karen, and I am here because the island represents a kind of experimental base for us. When I say "us," I am referring to the Frugal Innovation movement. We deal with reactivating public space and environmental self-help, for instance. I will explain more about that shortly.

But first some information about me. I grew up in the terribly conservative city of Winston-Salem in the terribly conservative state of North Carolina in a terribly conservative family. My father is a preacher at a Primitive Baptist church. We lived in a redbrick house dating back to 1805, which had probably never been properly aired since it was built. As a result, I was nearly always ill with bronchitis until I was twelve. Of course we all voted Republican in my family. Pa was a supporter of Newt Gingrich's total war and later a supporter of the Tea Party. The skin color of my friends had to be snow white. The cupboard with the Browning Automatics stood in the doorway. "The only defense you can rely on is self-defense," Pa used to say. He was always prepared for the worst.

I ran away to Detroit with a friend when I was seventeen and the first time I phoned home was on my eighteenth birthday. Because of that my brother Randolph hasn't spoken to me since. Detroit at first was all about going to parties. Nowhere else were there so many abandoned factories where people could lose it to the latest house music. Nevertheless, I managed to make up for lost time, passed the GED, and started to study urban planning. Of course this was because of Detroit. I was totally drawn to the decay, the empty skyscrapers, the grass growing over streets where rabbits, dogs, and junkies lived alongside each other.

One evening I got on the wrong bus. I was alone with a guy who all of a sudden went berserk and had the muzzle of a gun to my head for two stops. When the driver realized what was happening, he slammed on the brakes and the guy jumped out of the bus. The next few days I bawled my eyes out, and then I moved back south to Tampa with my boyfriend Friday. Tampa used to be adorned with signs that read "America's Next Great City." No other city was growing as fast or becoming rich as quickly. Homeownership meant awesome amounts of capital. Of course when we arrived we didn't have a home, and the "great city" dream had already run its course. Many people were living from flipping homes—meaning they bought up property in a poor condition, refurbished it a little, and sold it off one or two years later. In good times they could make a 50-percent profit. But those days were over now. Tampa had gone downhill. People could no longer pay their mortgages and went bankrupt. Think about that for a minute: in 2009 one and a half million Americans declared bankruptcy while the banks were paying their top managers bonuses worth millions from the very tax dollars that the government had pumped in to rescue them from collapse, and from the disaster that these top managers had caused. Wall Street dodged a bullet, while Tampa and the rest of America went to the dogs. Friday and I had had enough. We first made our way to East Africa working for a charity and distributed computers that were no longer needed in the States. But the villages in Rwanda and Tanzania had no stable power supply, the customs officials wanted bribes before we could import the computers, and the local assistance caused us more problems than the mosquitos.

Then we went to India. In Tamil Nadu there was a village where almost every inhabitant was a slave. The farmers could not pay back debts and worked on their creditor's estate for nothing. It turned out that the people owed the extortioner a total of ninety-one dollars. Sixty-four people were turned into slaves because of a sum that was less than a hundred bucks! We couldn't believe it …

But what we also realized in Africa and India was that people were able to survive on very little. The Africans walked around in sandals with soles made from moped tires. The Indian fishing boats consisted of something that looked like a large bean pod, six wooden poles, and a sail. They went out to sea like this, as their

49

ancestors did a few thousand years ago. Not to sound cynical, but it's true: poverty is the mother of invention.

Silicon Valley has certainly not gained a monopoly on creativity. Creativity is also present in fishing villages in India, Africa, and Latin America. Creativity with lots of money is certainly not very difficult. Creativity without money seems to be more interesting, in my view.

The movement for Frugal Innovation emerged from this interest. Learning from the poorest of the poor means arming ourselves for the future. We faced the challenge of transferring knowledge, techniques, and a culture of frugality from East to West and South to North. To achieve this we needed a place to try out this transfer process—a kind of relay station.

The island has become the relay station for us. We rely on cooperation with the state here. Why? Because this state serves the public sector. Streamlined bureaucracy and zero corruption. After all, the island itself is a laboratory. So it makes sense to test our ideas on frugality in pilot projects. If they prove successful, we can implement a project in sites in the outside world. The need is now so great that we can find partners anywhere.

The island is like a sheltered workshop. After all, we are working with fresh resources. Things look very different outside. More and more people are unable to cope. The state has turned its back on them and aid agencies are overwhelmed. We are a small group helping people in need to reinvent their everyday lives. With Frugal Innovation techniques. We're not going to save the world, but we are spreading a new concept.

Enough about me and why I'm on this island. I'll present our strategy later, along with a few of our pilot projects.

Lazaros

Yesterday I stopped being one of the printless. I know that from our social trainer. The printless used to be the paperless. People who couldn't prove their identity, or who destroyed their ID so they wouldn't have to. Some of them disappeared over the border to try their luck somewhere else. Today it's not your passport that matters, but your fingerprints. Once they're in the system, you can't escape. They call it biometric identification. It's like nature's stamp lets them monitor their little lambs.

Until yesterday my fingerprints were unsecured. That barely ever happens. You can't throw your fingerprints away like a piece of paper, you can just make them unreadable. But they've identified me now. The whole thing was for nothing. If I'd had the money, I would've gone to a friend in Salonika to get new prints. Apparently it's pretty easy, but too expensive. So I cut my fingers myself. Not just the thumbs, but all fingers of both hands, really deep zigzags, so that it really looked like an accident. It took three months for it to scar over. I almost didn't get to depart from Gavdos. We'd planned to do it at the new moon.

They have scanned my fingers four times in the last six weeks. That's how long I've been in this home. They call it a home and it is really one. You live in a room with four beds, a kitchen and bathroom in the hallway. I have a lot more space than at home in Nea

Moudania. And the food is better too. They're sending the scans to the police in other countries. If you think about it, it's a pretty easy job. Since Africans don't come here anymore, they only have to ask the countries to the north. You can see that I'm from there anyway. Now they all have the system with the fingerprints. It's only a matter of time before they snag you.

Cutting my fingers was a waste of time. Not only that, but the money's down the drain. Demi's too. My fingers don't hurt anymore. But losing the money does. Mainly because of Demi. I was the one to persuade her that it'd be best for her and the baby if we came here. And that we wouldn't make it if I didn't come over first in the rubber dinghy. And we needed all our cash for that. Even the money she got from her father when he died. And now they've identified me. They'll send me back. Just like they send back every-one who isn't a political and comes from the north. Everyone comes from the north. None of them are politicals.

So why is the trainer so civil? Of course they guess that the scars are a fake. I mean, that they're not an accident. He's not hounding us pointlessly. Running along the beach a bit is actually fun. I also have three hours of English a day. I can now understand most of the lyrics from Rabbit Junk, my favorite band. The five guys that I brought with me in the boat are already back home. That's how fast it happens. Two were Bulgarians. I found that out when I got here. I was the only uniden-tified. Until yesterday. There must be three hundred of us in this home. Everyone hoping, everyone waiting. All of us will have to leave sooner or later.

But a few people are allowed to stay. Even though they could send each of us back. The trainer says those who are honest and have an interesting skill get a chance. They do interviews. If you're good, they roll out the red carpet for you. I've got to stick with the trainer. I can't go back to Demi and tell her that everything went wrong. And what would happen to the baby? The trainer is not just civil, he's also curious. Pretty interested. He asked me earlier how we tricked the coastguard over there. I'm sure he knows exactly how and is only testing to see if I tell him the truth. But it wasn't very difficult. I told him everything, except about the guy who had a dinghy for sale with a 40 hp engine in the Korfos boondocks. I told him how I got enough food and water for three days and the other guys got 100 liters of fuel, the GPS, and the life jackets. The boat was not even four meters long. We just barely fit on board. The most remote part of Gavdos is an empty rocky beach with a huge hole in the rock where the sea comes in. We hid our cruise liner there on the beach until it was dark enough.

We rowed the first few kilometers. The stars were out, but it was hard to see anything. We had to keep an eye out for the lighthouse, but stayed close to the shore so that we stayed beneath the beacon. Then on to Gavdopoula. After I had switched on the engine and the boat was plowing through the water pretty smoothly, I felt really good. The smallest gust of wind would've sent us overboard. I stayed completely calm. The cold didn't bother me. Neither did the stench after three of the others threw up, one after the other.

The only problem was the cash. And the non-stop hitchhiking, first to Saloniki and then to Piraeus. These days hardly anybody picks you up. No idea why. Maybe they were afraid of us. We walked at least two hundred kilometers. All in all it took eight days. Then there was the ferry. One of the guys had to be smuggled on board. I guess he had even less dough than me. Still, you can never be sure.

The trainer seemed to like my story. We kept sitting after lunch in the canteen and I gave him all the details, including Demi and the baby. After all, he knows everything about us from the cops over there anyway. That we all live at my parents' house. My brother and my sister's family are living there too. Twelve people in four rooms. And sure, he figures that I like talking to him because I want to stay.

He asked me what kind of jobs I did. I thought he was joking. When have I known anybody around my age in Nea Moudania who works? Then he asked me what trade I had learned. Right, sandal-maker. My grandfather had a workshop in Saloniki. His speciality was Greek sandals. Dancing shoes. Even the opera was one of his customers. Apparently nobody was as good at making these things as he was. They are very simple. A low heel and a strap as thick as your finger. He always said it depended on the leather. Anyway, he always had the right sort. After I finished school I started an apprenticeship with him. But business wasn't so good. The opera and all his other customers had started ordering the trash from the Internet. The old guy kept warning me not to stay with him, saying nobody wanted handmade dancing sandals anymore.

He drilled the message into me. We tried it some more for a little while, and I was pretty good in the end. But nobody was buying anymore. He died at some point. I'd already left the workshop by then. I tried working as a signalman on the railway. Like my father. But that wasn't for me. Nothing was for me.

The trainer knew this too. But I told him anyway. Maybe he'll help me get an interview. He told me that artisans were in demand. That people here wanted to buy real things again. And then he said something else. Making shoes was a bit like art. The island was doing something for artists. Even if they didn't earn money sometimes. The island gave them a studio and board. They had earned this through their art.

Maybe I'll classify myself as an artist. But they already have me identified. I'm trying to remember the name of the stuff that my grandfather used to glue the upper part and the sole. It had an Italian name. Almost like Ferrari. Certainly he'll tell me tomorrow how things will proceed. If they'll proceed. Why would they make me learn English otherwise? I'll soon find out. Maybe Rabbit Junk was right: *This life is where you get fucked.*

Fabio 2

Although I grew up in Brazil and England, I also had Portuguese citizenship. But I only knew Portugal from the perspective of an Eton student who entered surfing competitions with his cousins, whom I hardly knew otherwise, during the summer break. I went, for instance, only to Lisbon twice to visit these same cousins and their family. The last time was about twenty-five years ago.

For twenty-five years I basically had no link to Portugal. My passport had expired without me noticing it. But Portugal suddenly remembered me in 2012. A huge loan from Brussels had just rescued the country from collapse and now a drastic search began for the guilty ones. Politicians are always accused first in these kinds of situations. Since you cannot expect them to fix the situation, it is easy for them to direct suspicion at those whom they can milk: the rich.

Portugal was not the only country in Europe that made its fellow countrymen living abroad responsible for its domestic crisis. This species, if they had cash, had the reputation of being doubly disloyal: they were indifferent to the fate of their country and paid their taxes elsewhere, if they did so at all. So just like France and a few other countries, Portugal switched to setting its sights on its citizens living abroad. Suddenly a law was passed that meant that the Portuguese were no longer taxed based on their place of residence, but according to their passport.

In the future, this law would have meant that I would have had to pay taxes in three different countries—Brazil, England, and Portugal—and possibly additionally in the countries where I was living at the moment with my family and where my children went to school. I would have had to reconcile my income and property with four or possibly more legistations, although these legislations not only failed to agree with each other, but also were contradictory, such as in delicate cases like the intergovernmental demarcation of both corporations and individuals.

So Betty and I, like thousands of others in a similar situation, started looking for places where we could have some peace and quiet away from the hungry taxmen, in our case the Portuguese. The catalogue of these places is no longer very long, ever since the world launched a campaign against tax havens and offshore centers. We did not want to spend the rest of our lives on a palm beach in the Caribbean, surrounded by a bunch of other refugees and a few thousand letter-box companies and banks, with infrastructure consisting of no more than an airfield, a villa resort, and a cinema for the domestic personnel.

What the island offers is quite different. For instance, immigration is actively welcomed. In Dubai, Monaco, or the Virgin Islands, nobody is interested in potential civic loyalty. Here, new citizens are supposed to arrive on the island as economic entities as well. The naturalization of people and assets is not just a new trick for gaining access to the riches of people who are wandering through the world without a home, as is the case in Great Britain, rather it turns private capital into a local economic force again. Money is not dead capital, but can be put to work on the island and elsewhere in the world. Anybody who decides to come to the island is automatically making a decision about the future of his or her economic activities. These people may remain players in global commerce, but in terms of capital economy, they land on the sovereign principality with a large portion of their assets. Imported capital is not just deposited in a numbered account, but is invested in real production. I admit that this impressed me.

I sold the trading company almost six months after my father's death to avoid the new demands from

Portugal. If I may say so, I still consider that the deal made at the time was fair to the buyer. The rubber and coffee business is as healthy as it was ten years ago— our plantations in Cambodia in particular are not only profitable, they are also grounded in a stable social consciousness. Three months later we received our new passports and naturalization papers for the first three years. So we moved to Lavapolis.

Dasha 1

Today marks the fifth anniversary of our arrival. Of course I still remember it like it was yesterday. It was dark when we left the airport. I took a few photos from the taxi. People moving around behind lit windows. A woman stood at a door, a green neon light behind her, one hand on her hip, a cigarette in the other. Flashes in the night. Dark messages for the arrivals.

Not that I wouldn't have understood any of these messages. I understood somewhat. The woman said something to me. That's why I haven't forgotten her or the cigarette in her hand. I'd finally stopped smoking in Austria because it was impossible as a smoker not to look like a criminal. That'd cost me nerves and three kilos weight. But I was already nervous anyway and Sergei, my ex-husband, said I was so thin you could see through me. Then suddenly this woman was standing there on my way from the airport to the short-term rental. As if she was holding out her cigarette for me. As if she wanted to tell me that they are not as strict here as over there on the continent. Not as strict as I had imagined. That I shouldn't worry about anything.

I was much calmer after the taxi ride than when I'd gotten in. Now things were really gonna start, and what exactly that meant for Ilyusha and me, even the night couldn't tell. Anyway I just sent the boy to the concierge for help in carrying our bags. And the concierge came and helped. That's how things are here, I thought to myself. Something I still think today.

Some say that the island is a paradise. Others say it's a paradise of evil. Both are right and wrong. There's a lot of turmoil in the world. But still, I'm not sure. From my office window I can't see any palm trees or the "evergreen sea," as they call it in some of the brochures. Everyone knows that nothing stays the same, not even the color of the water. I look out onto a rocky riverbed just before it flows out into the sea, which is hidden behind some apartment buildings. Every afternoon at the strike of three a woman with some kind of sheepdog wades out to a motorcycle skeleton stranded in the gravel. It washed up after a storm in the mountains last year. Storms happen here too. She wades out to the rusty motorcycle heap, strutting her hips, and back to the bank again. Even from here you can see that something's wrong with her. And the shaggy mutt does not exactly make the scene any more respectable. Maybe she's waiting for a john. I can see the arm of a plastic chair between the ferns. Anyway, every afternoon at three, if I happen to look out of my office window, I think it could've happened to me. And that it's happened to hardly anyone here. Maybe not even her.

II. At the Same Time

Simone 3

They tell us that mobility is freedom. Their thinking revolves around growth. Their polemics are directed against any doubts about the usefulness of acceleration. They are the unconditional speed merchants in absolute space. But ever since Einstein, we know that space is not absolute. I know all about the deceptive nature of speed. I say, the faster things go, the less progress we make. The more we chase after the future, the more ephemeral it becomes. We live in a hyperventilating era. It is unpredictable. It sweeps through time like a tornado. It snatches everything that is germinating and turns it into shabby, colorful waste in the twinkling of an eye. This voracious present is being sold as the future and is being acted out against the background of our fading memories. It gains its momentum from the multitude of living beings, from the domination of the living over the dead.

I am trying to escape it. But it's always there when I try to move myself out of harm's way. Only when I stand still do I sense what it is like to have escaped from this present. The island is this kind of standstill. A place where the dead can be remembered, where alternative time can be invented.

Stascha 2

The golden beach under my feet had been wearisome ever since the baccarat players returned for another Moët. A striking number of them were speaking my native tongue, and the overenthusiasm of these youth with regard to the superlatives of their holiday destination is enervating. My anger drove me to take action and I squeezed into my rented Renault Twizy (the island only has electric cars). Driving along perfectly maintained roads, past well-tended parks, rows of renovated houses, bustling shopping centers, and numerous zealously managed building sites, I realized that my expectation was confirmed that life here is outwardly comfortable . However, I inevitably returned to the question of how this is feasible so close to the social chaos elsewhere in the Mediterranean. Time has not only been shifted here. The island has both the world's highest standard of living and the lowest unemployment rate. The education and health systems have a reputation for setting standards, and the ratio of foreigners (almost 80 percent) has not caused any apparent cultural tension so far. At least that's what international surveys and the country's own propaganda brochures indicate, and what initially strikes even a critical eye.

These achievements are attributed to the shrewd policies of the so-called patron, Faidon. Admittedly, laws forbidding money laundering have been passed since the end of the casino economy. They have even triggered reforms in the worlds of trade and finances, which superficially regulate offshore business. That should have led to a drastic cut in public revenue and local prosperity. But it hasn't! What's going awry here?

The new laws may have driven out a few mafia bosses, drug dealers, and oligarchs, but they have not changed the outlandishness of the system itself.

Different tricks are hiding behind the reforms and they are even more cunning than those that good old Theodore might have dreamed up. Let's just take the latest invention, the immigration law: over the past two years island citizenship has been made available for purchase by anyone around the world! Price tag: half a million euros. Apparently there have been several thousand applicants from France, Russia, Italy, Great Britain, and Germany alone, and we only learn about most of them after they have been successfully finalized, as the new-fledged islanders begin the phaseout of their previous nationality. What is this noble Faidon trying to do? Set a good example? Or perhaps grab the greatest profits that can be obtained from the current crisis? No, it is impossible to sugarcoat the cynicism of a law that allows the superrich to purchase a foreign passport for what in their eyes is a small fee so that they can shed their own unbeloved citizenship and the associated tax obligations—even with the argument that these superrich pay a capital tax when they settle on the island and have to invest some of their assets in local gold beaches.

The true nature of the immigration saga is only comprehensible if you look behind the facade of what seems to be such a peaceful brand of multiculturalism. Boundless profits are still available from exploiting low-wage earners who are recruited with false promises from the inexhaustible reservoirs of Africa and South Asia. It is a slave market that still makes use of those routes that supplied the island with the raw material for its parasitic wealth in the centuries preceding the era of the volcano's eruption.

In contrast to the dismal times of Genoan naval supremacy, which used the island as the hub between the so-called Christian and Muslim worlds, the current masters are no longer traders, but purchasers. The army of tens of thousands of helots from India, the Philippines, Pakistan, Angola, Nigeria, and again of late—as was the case in the days of the late Theodore—southern Europe, are creating an ongoing economic miracle for a privileged caste of islanders and the international circle of crisis profiteers. But that does not make the practice any less dubious. These men and women are fleeing the misery of their domestic work situation in the hope of a better livelihood on a foreign island and are tied down by high agency fees and anti-employee clauses. Once they have been muzzled, they slog their way through the almost endless workday on scaffolding or as maids in posh manor houses. Herded together in mass accommodation, where the old Messinis used to accommodate his Greek guest workers, they are locked away from the intrusive gaze of wary visitors.

I have read the reports by Human Rights Watch. People have apparently been dismissed in breach of contract. From one day to the next workers fell into complete poverty and material dependence on those who had provided the money for the job placement and the trip. Without any rights, they were deported immediately, partly because it was feared that some might commit suicide …

An excavation site was right ahead. To spare the tires, I parked the electric car carefully on the tuff-sealed shoulder between two oleander bushes and tried to spot a few of the poor wretches. The Twizy thermometer indicated thirty-six degrees. Just barely tolerable. Apart from three huge excavators lowering their shovels in a pit and dumping loads onto a cone-shaped heap, there was not much to see. The men in the excavators are not white, as per usual, and wear lemon-yellow jackets and helmets.

I backed the Twizy onto the road. The term "human capital" develops its full bitterness here. These peons and their masters' grubby cash form part of the dark matter of this island. I will have to visit one of these worker camps.

First I had to cope with the traffic, which was becoming heavier. Nobody seemed to be in a hurry—at least no one sped past me on the right or flashed their lights at me from behind, as is usual in Mediterranean countries. Drivers even stopped at pedestrian crossings and at bus stops people waited for the bus in a friendly semicircular queue. But it is impossible to overlook the fact that both the people in electric vehicles and on the road are almost exclusively Asian, African, or white, having arrived here from distant lands. They are foreigners. After all, even the locals are foreigners here. That takes a bit of getting used to.

After a boring, stress-free half-hour drive, the residential development of Novo Lavapolis stretched out at the end of the four-lane boulevard (if the term "residential development" is not too modest in light of the two hundred and fifty thousand registered residents here). The main building complex looks from the distance as if Captain Kirk's spaceship *Enterprise* had landed here in 1969 after the end of the first series, and was then abandoned to the moods of the tides. But, it is viewed as *the* exclusive form of "a new way of living" in the eyes of the local property agents.

I was naturally wary and headed for a parking space in front of the complex, which arches monstrously over the coastline, and scouted around with hand raised to shield my eyes from the sun. The area had trimmed lawns, cacti, and channels set in stone, where quiet water now and then lapped against weirs, a children's playground, football fields, basketball courts, and a marina with probably a few hundred sailing boats that stretched out toward the gates that lead to the city of Lavapolis. Whatever the "new way of living" may be in this lagoon idyll, it is definitely exclusive. The local elite and the stateless multimillionaires live here next door to each other in a luxury social-housing complex. A starred restaurant, a tennis court, a theater, and a private school are just around the corner.

Apart from a few adolescents who were listlessly shooting hoops, none of the two hundred thousand fortunate people in Novo Lavapolis seemed to be interested in all these nice facilities. Or do people not want to be seen? I've read that a cunning electronic concierge system protects the residents from too much nosiness. That's a sign of reserve, which runs counter to the repeated declarations by the island government that people here live in an informal community without being tied to their material and social status. I considered the thought of entering the complex illegally, then abandoned it and got back into my Twizy. There is plenty to see on this island, and more than once did I have to rub my eyes in disbelief.

New garden-housing developments are springing up right behind the golf course in Lavapolis. You might be tempted to think that these are the same as in Doha, Miami, or the villa suburbs in Shanghai: megalomaniacal castles with the standardized tasteless design of the philistines from every country who have become rich too quickly.

Instead, there is a kind of vigorous post-Bauhaus style here: simple brick apartment buildings, as gray as the desert next door, with communal gardens and a community center. On the desk in my hotel room I'd seen the glossy projects of the real estate agents. But if you step beyond the threshold of this housing, which appears to be so unobtrusive on the outside, you become embroiled in the cool atmosphere of perfect high-tech design. The dominant themes here are the elegance of empty space and disguised nuance. At most there is a Picasso or a Calder hanging on the wall, but otherwise there is not even a television. The absence of any sense of splendor is more intrusive than the normal magnificence. It is hedonistic arrogance masked by frugality. This is what they want, these brigades of jaunty start-up entrepreneurs, marketers, and dentists from Mumbai, Istanbul, and Munich—cities they don't like anymore.

Alberto 3

Heterotopias do not have the assurance of being accepted outside of the political arena to which they belong. This also applies to our island. Patron Faidon has repeatedly—particularly because of our success—called for modesty and transparent arguments. We do not claim to have found the general solution for current and future economic problems.

I am still proud to have played a role in shaping our society from a privileged lookout. We introduced directly or in modified form many of the measures prepared in the Faidon/Martel research paper, despite international criticism and many objective difficulties. The related remodeling of foreign policy and local relations of production, the directional shift in social discourse or economic goals, fundamentally altered the face of the island and its culture. We have passed through various stages of a heterotopia in the meantime. Today our state may be viewed as a counter-site in the Faidon/Martel sense. It represents the outside world, as its citizens come from there, and it remains in almost unhindered political and economic contact with it. And it is leading the way for the outside world, in that it abandons traditional principles as soon as they run contrary to the interests of the island and its citizens.

As I already mentioned, modesty is one of the first civic duties on the island. Anybody who arrives here for the first time with an impartial view will not be particularly startled by iconic architecture or futuristic technology or loud colors at the malls or markets. The island is perhaps less colorful than most of its Mediterranean neighbors, particularly the urban centers. It is almost monochrome. There are a few gentle nuances of color provided by the sky and the earth and absorbed in the cultivated landscape. Against this backdrop a perpetual theater of physiognomies, languages, and gestures plays out. Newcomers discover a concentration of cultural differences not found anywhere else on so small a stage. At the same time they recognize an unwritten consensus among the islanders. They are the pioneers of a social experiment that they have selected for themselves.

According to our view at the Department of Strategic Planning, the pioneer consensus on our island is visible in the close relations between the territory and its political leaders. The island actually proves that politics always affects an inhabited area. State power, however, depends on its propagation in a territory. It needs mediality to prove itself. It discovers its limits wherever the voice of power doesn't reach. That was true of ancient Rome and the British Empire and it is true of this principality too.

This gives rise to a problem for government systems today with their intensely widespread information network: they are susceptible to a high communications risk. Their power has maybe spread in the virtual space of the global economy and popular culture. But anonymous mass societies no longer allow any individual relation between government power and its citizens. The latter belong to a virtual storehouse of information consumers. They no longer feel any loyalty toward the state.

This principality does not treat its citizens like microscopic particles of a larger mass. The citizens of this principality are the personification of an idea; they are the supporters of the idea of an alternative society. The islanders thus incarnate, with all their ethnic diversity, the medium of the power that predominates in the community. They belong here because of a free and individual decision. And as they have arrived on the island from all over the world and are still in touch with the world, they also disperse the idea of this experiment throughout the outside world.

Critics accuse us of being naive. They say, for example, that multiculturalism and social tolerance have failed. Perhaps that is true. But we are practicing a different politics: that of universal solidarity. The people on our island share what appears to be a paradox to those looking on from outside: they are at home in the world and yet protected from many affronts originating in this world. This feeling strengthens their pioneer spirit. Because it can only survive if it is spread, we shall pass it on from one generation to another.

Haruko 2

So I followed Lisa south to Goodshare. Admittedly, I'm still not living here officially. I can stay for up to three months with a European passport. Many people struggle along like this—they take a ferry to Malta, Sicily, or Crete every now and then, get their passport stamped, and come back. Of course the local authorities are aware of these tricks, but they're not bothered by them. An estimated thirty thousand Europeans and Americans, most of them under thirty, lead this semilegal island existence. Many have been doing it for years. They call us "Shadows" or "Yellows," because we are not really islanders, but still somehow belong. Since I'm half-Japanese and have to be careful about exposing my sensitive skin to the sun, I find both descriptions very apt. I use one of the Doraemon posters from the manga kissa in Berlin as a screensaver. Not for nostalgic reasons, but out of gratitude for having met Lisa there.

I started out as her assistant. I was allowed to look over her shoulder as she provided further training at the local trade school, and I gradually set up my own network. That's how I came in contact with the Common House project after barely two weeks on the island. I was offered a job as an architect for the first time since I had qualified at the Architectural Institute of Japan in Tokyo six years ago. And there was an apartment to go with it! There are manga kissas here too in fact, but I couldn't reject this offer. Instead of earning money, I worked for the first year's rent. I was already at home in the nonmonetary economic cycle.

Common House is a kind of social-housing project. The government leases the land to a local entrepreneur who promises to create communal apartments for a unit of two hundred residents. I was employed with a colleague from Lisa's Goodshare group to design a unit in Common House. This involved recycling and reusing as many demolished parts as possible from houses that are currently being knocked down next to the casino strip. Fortunately we've found a lot of timberwork that can be used to make simple residential structures, which will be covered by roof tiles. The designs are inspired by the traditions of my homeland. An *ie* is the smallest residential unit in Japan. *Ie* basically means a house. A Japanese mini-house consists of a shop (*mise*) and a bedroom (*nema*). Tokyo and other cities in my country are full of *ie* settlements. This combination of commercial and personal space, which maintains a sense of intimacy but also functions in a social sense, seemed to be well suited to Common House. Many people here operate small businesses too. It's not entirely like being at home, and not entirely like being out in public. This results in an obscure intermediate space where people can try out new ways of living. My employer gave the go-ahead for this experiment. He seemed to be certain we'd find plenty of people interested in participating. We've now built the first part of Common House—two units for four hundred tenants in total. We've designed 120 *ie*. Common House is already a funny labyrinth of these one-cell homes. A new city within the city of Lavapolis.

One of these *ie* is now my home, albeit unofficially. I have to abandon it for a few days at most every time my tourist visa is on the verge of expiring. Through the glass wall of the *mise*, which I use for my Goodshare work, I can see the neighbors strolling in the covered alleyway in front of my door or working in their *ie*. I rented the printer and desk with the apartment. There is a kind of sea crate in the *nema* for my clothes and a raised bed with a dining table underneath. I have stuck a poster showing the night sky in Tokyo over the bed. After all, I am one of the Yellows who haven't yet completely severed their ties with their old homeland.

Friday 2

Before we talk about ourselves, our activities, we need to talk about our predecessors. We have studied their strategies and projects in great detail in order to understand what we need to change.

What distinguishes us from earlier alternative movements? They failed due to two problems:

they lacked a clear perspective and a clear identity. These movements were always staged according to the same dramaturgy: initially they'd gather outside of society and then attack society from their marginalized position. They temporarily bid farewell to the conventions of a system in order to be able to criticize their contemporaries for these conventions. This status of standing outside of society was deemed to be a protest movement and was soon the trademark of alternative options. We can see a problem of perspective here. I'll come back to this later.

These movements took on the form of creative destruction à la Schumpeter. During the first phase, the alternatives pulled down a few walls of the existing system in the name of freedom. During the second phase, they built up new walls in order to defend their freedom. The protagonists of the movements often used one of two alternative career strategies and confirmed that they had questioned power in order to be able to exert it themselves. Some of them moved into the colorful world of popular culture, while others entered the colorful world of parliamentary politics. (A tiny minority dedicated themselves to the strategy of gray terrorism without any other alternative.) In excluding themselves from society, the majority of the alternatives were keen to return to the same society with grand sensation and eloquent reasoning. Rather like a child who runs away from the family home and is embraced all the more warmly upon returning.

Apart from melancholic memories and some martyrs, not much is left of the alternatives. We believe any effective criticism of society will either trigger a revolution, in order to be effective, or its critics should see themselves as part of this society. You can really see this dilemma in the fate of our predecessors. Their error was to think that you can decide of your own free will whether you want to be part of a society or not. The paradox of postwar society in Europe and the US was that individual freedom had prospered to such a degree that a new generation was able to help itself to the freedom of decrying the lack of freedom, with almost no resistance (in comparison to the attempts of previous generations).

The initial culture of self-criticism among the alternatives was just an imitation of Maoist procedures. They soon restricted themselves to making "the others" the target of their criticism. Their criticism was the self-righteous kind—along the lines of "You're doing it wrong, we're doing it right." Because they didn't question themselves, didn't criticize their own criticism or positions, their alternative remained an alternative within the existing system. And so they remained part of this system. The early environmentalists among them were no different. The message that they directed against an ecology-adverse society should have been directed against themselves too. The system proved to be greater and more comprehensive than the critics had thought. Occupying houses did not abolish ownership of property any more than riding bikes stopped the destruction of the environment. Free love did not eliminate rearmament. "Give me a place to stand and I will move the world," Archimedes supposedly said. The alternatives actually believed that this kind of place might exist.

We recall this political naïveté not without some sympathy. We are grateful for the commitment and the experience with which these people have enriched and inspired our own movement. We are also grateful that the Internet has liberated us from the political shortcomings of earlier movements. In the end, their commune was the footnote to the system, which continued for a further generation because their resistance was only temporary. Our community will become the pillar of a new system.

The Internet has cured us from all illusions of the usefulness of Archimedean places and politically marginalized positions. The Internet has taught us to view positions like inside and outside as relative positions, making it possible to handle the paradox that by criticizing society we also criticize ourselves. The Internet has taught us to think inclusively and bid farewell to the exclusiveness of earlier movements. The Internet has also taught us that inclusiveness should not be confused with the notion of community. Inclusiveness is the process of including yourself, not including others. We are taking action on ourselves before we direct our attention toward society. Our deed sets the example for the possible deeds of others. We are calling for involvement, not liberation.

Our group is not another attempt at creative destruction with the goal of erecting future walls according to our own building plans. We are not demanding power, but rather a general dissolution of boundaries. We are convinced that our social and cultural goals are identical with those of a great majority of the world's population. We are in the majority, but our influence is small. Politically, we are a growing power. The elite embody diminishing power. We have nothing to hide, but a great deal to share with each other. Our goal is a society that shares, not one that conceals.

Simone 4

I am prepared to sacrifice a settled lifestyle and therefore the classic right to public societal recognition. I am foregoing any place in this society. But I am very much here. The status of "being in transit" links me to the nomads, and the status of "being there" connects me to those that settle down.

I am not, however, a traditional nomad. Nomads follow trajectories that people like them have followed since long ago. They follow the rhythms of life in the landscape. Nomads do not have a home, but the topography of these rhythms is their home. Their life unfolds not in a locality but on a trajectory.

I am not sedentary and I am not itinerant. My home is a heterotopia with a thousand imaginary landscapes. My tracks take me through an air-conditioned shopping center today and through a retweet tomorrow. They pass through populated areas and describe the world as a linear flow of human and nonhuman figures. In this sense, they are similar to the cosmogonies of primitive peoples. But I am not aware of any benefactors of these orders. The journey is not the destination. It is only an option without any privileges. By treading many paths, I prove that space is neutral. Everybody has access, everything is permitted. Space is a buffer zone between the places where partisanship dominates. The island is, for example, the buffer zone between the places of the outside world. Those that exclude one another outside meet here. Those that are at war with one another outside negotiate here. Those that steal from one another outside trade here.

Padma 2

The first Malayalis arrived in the 1960s when the hotels on the strip needed personnel and the people from my country were clearly preferred at many establishments to Greeks, Turks, Tunisians, or southern Italians. Maybe because they were easier to exploit or could play the exotic card. The British Empire had just fallen and many a Lord So-and-So, who had blown his Bengal jewels in the Stardust, may have preferred to enjoy personal ruin in the presence of gentle Indian domestics. The official immigration statistics number more than one hundred thousand men and women from Kerala. They make up 20 percent of the total population and are the largest minority, ahead of the Chinese, Arabs, and Turks. They include representatives of the IT sector in Thiruvananthapuram, delegates from trading and textile companies in Cochin, medium-sized wholesalers and business people, teachers, managers, and employees of the huge multinational logistics companies in Container City.

All of these people quickly reached a reasonable level of prosperity and their families often followed them. They were fed up with the political unrest in the cities at home and turned their backs on the sit-ins, strikes, and protest marches used to force the central government or a few monstrously expanding monopolies to introduce better working and living conditions. It is amazing to see how people who have grown up with a Stalinist version of communism are now apparently learning the mechanisms of small-grade capitalism and professional competition with a sense of enthusiasm. They often knew nothing but the hopeless chaos in Kerala and suddenly come to terms with a service-based society. They are believed to have a genetic predisposition to a lack of respect and cynicism, but their arrival in the globalized island community is a success story. There are now so many of them that they represent every conceivable facet of the Malayali culture: all the nuances of religion, cults, political parties, castes, astrology, clans and cliques, universities, languages, and sects. The Malayalis have their clubs and events like any other national communities. They have their stores selling DC Books like the ones at home in Trivandrum and they read the papers and magazines published in Cochin and Dubai.

But there is a group of Malayalis who have not found reasonable prosperity and are not living here with their families. As guest and seasonal workers on a building site, they definitely earn more than their predecessors did a few years ago. They may enjoy union representation and live in individual accommodation in more comfortable surroundings than many illegal arrivals from Europe who have found shelter on the island. But they have not really made it here. My cousin Sujit is one of them.

Before I can tell Sujit's story, I need to talk about Mr. Xylouris. Mr. Xylouris is one of the second-generation building contractors on the island. His father was responsible for some of the cheap hotels on the strip, but the son learned from his mistakes and even created something like a new landmark for the island with Amari University. Two years ago Mr. Xylouris underwent a rejuvenation cure at a clinic in Ernakulam in Kerala. Mr. Xylouris chose this destination because he wanted to keep a promise that he had made to his foreman Sujit: to visit him in his South Indian home one day. Sujit lives outside Ernakulam on a hill with several acres of land. His family uses the land to grow coffee beans.

Mr. Xylouris was amazed. His foreman owned a larger house than he did, and furthermore, there were the extensive plantations. His young and attractive wife and four children spoke fluent English and even knew all about the distant island belonging to Patron Faidon since they spent their last summer holidays there. Their Mediterranean visitor was granted opulent hospitality. He soon felt years younger in Sujit's house, even before heading to the spa cure in Ernakulam.

Before Mr. Xylouris returned home, he asked to talk to Sujit in private. He confessed to his foreman that he was ashamed to have him live in such poor conditions on the island, although Sujit was obviously more prosperous than him. Mr. Xylouris said he could not understand why Sujit worked in a hard and moderately paid job thousands of kilometers from home and spent his lonely evenings in a tiny room when his life was so much better in India. He added that it would of course be a disadvantage for the business to lose such a good man, but if Sujit no longer wanted to return to the island, he could perfectly well understand and was ready, albeit regretfully, to do without him.

Fear suddenly filled the face of the man from India. He told his boss that a coffee bean on the island was worth just as much as a coffee tree on his plantation in Kerala. He said his generous employer needed to understand that his modest life on the island was the flipside to his good fortune in India. If he abandoned his job, he would also lose his home in Kerala.

Xenia

He ruined us with his rotten ideas. His historians call him his father's favorite son. But he was the black sheep of the family. First of all, he drove out his older brother, then betrayed his father. He first brought shame on his family and then on the whole principality. The governments of great nations have now described his crazy rulership, which has now continued for thirty years, as a threat to democracy and economic stability.

They say that we are money launderers and conceal terrorists, that we are diplomatic cheats and corrupters of humankind. Those are the rewards for arrogance and maltreating the world with political lunacy, for playing the role of missionary when you your-self have renounced your faith.

He first and foremost renounced his faith. In Paris. He surrounded himself with homosexuals, athe-ists, and drug addicts. His doctrine of this modernistic heterotopia is nothing other than a modernistic mari-juana cloud. The main thing was to be different—that's all that mattered. He'd hardly taken over his father's throne when he changed the Orthodox calendar. As if it wasn't bitter enough when the patriarchy of

Constantinople rejected the Julian calendar a hundred years earlier. But we were still one with our brothers and sisters in the old calendar church when it came to our most important holiday celebrating Christ's crucifixion and resurrection. But that was naturally too much for our enlightened master and his heathen friends from Paris. For thirty years now we have been disconnected from Easter as it's celebrated by the holy men on Mount Athos. And he celebrates this barbaric act every year as a symbol of reunification with the Western Church. As if it was his business. As if relations with the Catholics were his province.

But Europe has not thanked him for it. Nothing has: not the rejection of America, not the new tax laws. What he calls independence is really isolation—the removal of Washington's strong hand, the expulsion of Vegas fever, the loss of our old friends, of their influence and money.

I was born on this island and will soon be put into its earth. Just like my father and my mother, who were among the early settlers. We were there when the first water pipe was laid or when the lads from the Sixth Fleet stormed the Stardust. Charlton Heston, Lollobridgida, George Marshall—they were all here. They lionized us as the "Miracle with the Strip." We were the Miracle with the Strip! I can still hear the cries of the gulls, accompanied by the saxophones in the casinos, when, on the arm of my late husband (Makis was his name), I strolled along the pier. I can still see the protest signs on the waterfront, "Fingers Off Our Strip!" People had secretly set them up during the night after he announced the demolition.

He destroyed the strip and drove away the miracle. He tampered with the constitution. Our men are not even allowed to take up arms anymore. We are now a "heterotopia." He is a master of inventing words. Words cloak the chaos and the betrayal. Dictatorship of the foreigners—that's what it should be called.

His father had created a society that was absolutely unique. The old culture of our seafaring peoples and the humble Orthodox faith had fused with the American way of life on this island. We were rather like the Mediterranean frontier and the people who came to us knew this and appreciated it. They valued our conservatism because it was unique in Europe. They appreciated our liberalism, our family values, and our legal claim to self-defense.

Those who arrive now value the Social Fund—the provision for people who have failed to be successful anywhere else and are now our burden. This flood of Arabs that are fighting each other in their own countries. And these starvelings from Europe who annoy us with their alternative ideas and their inclusiveness. He has enchained them through the Social Fund; and they are more than happy to be enchained. They are not cut from the same cloth as the first generation of settlers. Back then they were not subordinate to the state, but to the patron. But the patron was not looking for subjects. Rather, he was looking for men who were driven by their own will and who, with all the means in their power, wanted to adopt this island as their own. We always had foreigners on the island—we, the natives, were the minority. But in his father's day, it was easy to distinguish the foreigners.

They came here to amuse themselves and then they left. Today they come to stay. There are now so many of them that they can resoundingly outvote us. They can determine our lifestyle.

Babylon would be the right name for the island. Confusion created by polyglot vagrants and starvelings. These characters, weeded out elsewhere, have allowed themselves to be abused as extras in his modernistic heterotopia. Those who sleep with the dogs should not be surprised if they wake up with lice. If these people had known something about culture at home, they lost it on their way here. They are all trying to be global players. Their background does not play a role anymore. Once they've been uprooted, they'll enjoy a cheap meal wherever they get it. These people only feel at home once all distinctions have been abolished. Then they won't be discriminating anymore. Equality turns into indifference. Most important is that the junk-food temples are not far off and that you can buy the usual rubbish and have something amusing to tell people. "Oh, sweetheart, this sunset is just like the one in Tenerife last week! And the Louis Vuitton bag is even cheaper here than at the airport in Abu Dhabi!" Only here the employer is much more generous than elsewhere. If you are cunning about it, you don't need to hold down an employment or register with the authorities. You can bum along without being disturbed.

I only go outside when I go to the doctor's. It's impossible to find your way around here. Every week they build new roads. You can't rely on your own eyes, or on the GPS in your car either. I could work as a travel guide in a lost city: Here you can see a few broken bricks from the first homes on our island, fired barely seventy years ago and most likely plowed down by bulldozers tomorrow. And behind the construction fence is the pit my childhood school has disappeared into.

Things can't happen quickly enough under the regime of Sir Mr. Son. He is confusing speed with progress. He wants to make us believe that we are living in a new social system. How can you create a society at this mad pace? You can build houses, but not people. You can pass laws, but you cannot legislate a lifestyle. They preach social development and only want a little bit of space in the sun. The final cry of the strategists is neutrality. As if we had not always been independent. As if the Americans had not let us pursue our own path from the outset. What they call neutrality is nothing more than indifference—indifference to the needs of the island population and even indifference to the new arrivals. Indifference is a vicious circle. People are not interested in each other—this is the new feature of this society. In the past, people used to see each other at mass on the weekend because they still shared the same faith. But those days are over. They now have this ridiculous museum shack with the chic name "Agora."

The rulers stubbornly remain neutral, particularly when it comes to their own history. There is hardly a word of respect for the father. What we are, we are thanks to our own absolute power and brilliant ideas. There is no time for historical justice.

The few of us who have carefully retained our memories of the island as it was a few decades ago are not extremists. We are not right wing or left wing. We are islanders. Many of us have left because we can no longer stand life here. Others have become old and have been able to forget. They have even been able to forget to die. Others have been finally redeemed. A few thousand of them have been buried. But they are only a small fraction in comparison to the number of those who live here now. There are at least twelve living for every one that's died. How can the dead make themselves heard in the face of the stifling majority of those stomping around on their soil? How can we prevent all traces of sacrifice and courage from being wiped out in the near future? They are talking these days about a new culture. But they haven't once understood that culture starts with the dead and ends with the dead—a concern therefore of only a small minority on our island. What will happen with the dead and with their concern, when the majority is not interested in the interests of the minority?

Karen 2

Here is an excerpt from the Manifesto of Frugal Innovation: "This movement stands for handling natural and man-made resources in an ascetic way. We develop, promote, and practice Frugal Innovation. The island is our ideal object for field research. We are following the creation of a society as it happens. We comment on and influence the creation of a political and cultural order.

"In their early phases, economies are often greedy, unscrupulous consumers of workers, energy, and raw materials. Maximum exploitation is the means to accumulate power and capital. It is therefore our goal to break through the vicious circle of unrestrained consumerism and obsessively profit-oriented production on the island. Economic development and ecological respect are not opposed to each other, in our view. There are numerous opportunities for handling resources in an improvised manner. We call this Frugal Innovation.

"Frugal Innovation covers all the ideas and techniques that do not use massive amounts of material resources and that provide broad spectrums of the population with a respectable standard of living. For a long time the ecology movement was a luxury domain of an elite class of fairly wealthy people in industrial nations. Concern for the environment first became vocal only after concern for material prosperity had been assuaged.

"Global recognition of dramatic climate change offers the chance to turn the tables. We are convinced that material well-being is impossible without ecological well-being. We represent the view that Frugal Innovation points the way to a postconsumer society. Solidarity, asceticism, and prevention are some of the highest values.

"When looking more closely at the economic and social development in the second half of the twentieth century, it is clear that this era has been characterized by two kinds of peace—an inner and an outer peace. The nations of the world granted themselves the latter through balancing global threats. Technological innovation was stimulated by the arms race.

"Inner peace was initially the product of a social contract, which gradually has been eroded by the stakes of mass consumerism. The waste products of military-technical innovations stimulated the purchasing power of a global consumer society weary of politics.

"This double peace was purchased by a senseless arms race and the total mobilization of commercialism. It is therefore no wonder that this era does not provide us with any lessons to arm us for the fundamentally new tasks of the prevention society.

"The economies of scarcity, politically excluded from the global community, and the culturally incompatible pariah nations are our sources of ideas with their obscure experiences of informal survival practices and feasibility techniques. Many of the Frugal Innovation projects introduced below are based on the quiet, secret wisdom of starving, humiliated people in countries like Cuba or North Korea.

"Activists belonging to our movement distribute aid beneath the radar of global embargos to thousands of peasants in almost inaccessible regions who would otherwise go without food. They help these poor, crushed people to establish some modest infrastructure. And they are learning how these people have maintained the gift of technical improvisation in their utter hopelessness. The prevention society of the future will owe its progress in Frugal Innovation to this inheritable talent."

Dasha 2

The best view of the island is from Point Alpha, the basalt ledge on the volcano. People simply call the volcano Bouno, the mountain. It is the only elevation on the island, but still takes up quite a lot of space. It looks like a small mountain range. I drove out to Raches this afternoon and took the railway to Point Alpha. Every guidebook for people entering the country mentions Point Alpha. It is an unwritten law that you should visit the lookout point after arriving. And then again on anniversaries. I actually often go there for professional reasons. I work in the immigration office, in the department for illegal immigration. Twice a week I bring my candidates, who are among the Yellows, up there to show them the island. That is part of their preparation work for the examination.

There is always something new to see from Point Alpha. Lavapolis continues to grow out into the sea every month. Like a bushy anemone that has suddenly appeared out of the water—glistening and slippery, green and gray, a labyrinth with thousands of veins and openings. Dried-out wadis fill the ragged desert basin in the middle of the island. The angular geometry of the motorways and railway tracks. The demolition site next to the casino strip with the crooked metal comet tail on the roof of the Stardust, forever releasing trails of dust—like a sign that the wild stars of yesteryear are long gone and the old times are finally over.

Green, yellow, and gray. From up there it looks as if these colors make up the whole island. If the weather is clear and the light at an angle, you can see the beaches at three points of the compass. To the west are sandy coves and sharp-edged lava fields flecked with windswept broom shrubs, and between, the airport with its three terminals and Container City with its various docks. On the other side are the new Amari University and Knowledge City. The patron had them built on the eastern bank because the sun should rise over the academics.

The scree from Bouno comes to Point Alpha from the north. The most recent is just about seventy years old, and when the sun is setting you can clearly see where the material turned cold and came to a stop. They are assuming that the volcano will remain dormant for at least another two hundred years. But they haven't tried to build anything on the sides of Bouno. There are ecological arguments against doing so nowadays, but nobody bothered about those twenty years ago. For whatever reason, the mountain remained untouched.

At this time of the year the sun sets to the right, behind Terminal Beta, and leaves a red trail for a few minutes on the smooth sea, as if a burning rocket was drilling into the depths. As soon as the trail has disappeared, a network of lights descends over the island, and over the beaches out to sea. Concrete skeletons turn into white lamp cages. Although nobody has been able to build higher than eight stories for a few years now, these building sites remind me of the Seven Sisters in Moscow, the high-rise blocks from the Stalin era, which no longer seem to be so monstrous nowadays.

That afternoon on Point Alpha I imagined that I could see the red-blue neon sign of the Carrefour supermarket in Segment Five, our district in Lavapolis, where I do my bulk shopping on Saturdays. Actually it's impossible, because my eyes are not very good anymore. When my mother died twenty years ago and—having just reached legal age, with Sergei on my hands and Ilyusha in my tummy—I had to share the apartment on Gogol Boulevard with a married couple, I would not have dreamed it possible to have a living space of eighty square meters on my own. That is the size of our flat. Of course, eighty square meters isn't that fantastic. We had more than one hundred in Tel Aviv and we definitely had at least ninety in Salzburg too.

But here with two and a half rooms, two people who have very different and sometimes antagonistic needs, like Ilyusha and I, manage very well. That wasn't the case before with his father. Not only because of the shared living space, but that did have something to do with it. What is standard in Lavapolis is exorbitant luxury anywhere else. Standard apartments in Segment Five guarantee at least 50 percent of available sunshine each day. That is about five times higher than in Moscow. The light is UV-filtered, of course. Noise insulation between the rooms is also very efficient. Ilyusha has played the marimba for two years, but I only can hear it if he lets me into his room.

In Tel Aviv we spent the days with the blinds down and in Salzburg it was foggy or the sky was gray. And you could hear everything. The bathroom was a kind of acoustic letter shoot set vertically through the entire building. In Israel we didn't even need an alarm clock because the commuters started driving past our house at six in the morning.

We get along well with each other. Ilyusha is now fourteen. He speaks four other languages alongside Russian, one of which is Hebrew. Perhaps he will win the fencing championship this year. Perhaps he will become a musician. The father of one of his friends is a former Formula 1 star and the mother of another friend is a former supermodel. For many people the island is their "next step." But not for us. For us it's just our "now." But there are also many normal people in Ilyusha's world and I suspect that the boy is not particularly impressed by one side or the other. Yes, he will make his own way—and still know when he should listen to his mother.

Ordinary mortals who apply for official residence here have to pass a blood test and an entrance exam. They ask you about your career, your political views, what you know about the island, the prince, its economic significance, and its history. First of all you need to have taken a good look around the job market and make sure you know about the Social Fund. If you have no job prospects, your future looks bleak. And then there is a seemingly innocuous question that is actually quite crucial. I am very familiar with this procedure for professional reasons. I know when they will ask the question, I know what kind of answer they expect from the different types of people and the influence the answer has on the exam result. But already back then, over five years ago, when I flew here excited and with mixed feelings after many futile attempts to leave Europe and was subjected to this test, I suspected that the way I answered this question would determine my fate. How do you imagine your life and that of your son in five years? That was the seemingly innocuous question.

All things considered, my response worked: Ilyusha will be healthy and will go to a good school, I will have a decent job, and we will live on this island because life will be better for us here, not because it would be worse somewhere else.

Fabio 3

For a few minutes this morning, the lawn behind the house was white. Jamie, our youngest, danced among the snowflakes with his tongue out like a shaman shortly before he takes on a different form of being. He is two years old and has never seen snow before. According to the news, this is something he shares with the entire island.

My father would have taken that as a reason for making fun of the environmentalists. He has not missed an opportunity during the last few years to talk with palatable irony about "global warming" whenever the weather was too cold for the season. This winter he would've had a lot of fun. We are experiencing temperatures like those in the north. Particularly amusing for him would have been the fact that the meteorologists immediately come up with explanations that underpin their theory of climate change. Of course they can't get by without some paradoxes. For instance, the current cold weather is due to the fact that the polar ice caps are melting. Less ice means stronger solar radiation in the sea, which means that the air is heated to a greater extent, which means a change in thermals ... and the forecasters say that it's only logical that we are experiencing cold and rain. The logic is absurd.

I was six when I saw snow for the first time. We had moved to London from Belo Horizonte in Brazil a few weeks earlier. The house in Belgravia had a garden too, and one morning it was white. I took a cup from the kitchen table, scooped up the strange stuff from the lawn, and eagerly put it in my mouth. It was a huge disappointment, because I was firmly convinced that candy floss had fallen from the sky overnight. My father, who grew up in Brazil like me, must have experienced a similar trauma as a boy, since a few days later he took me to one of the large railway stations in London and bought me some real candy floss.

Three generations, all sharing one childhood experience. You might think that the world had remained pretty much the same, despite climate change. But in reality, my old man and I lived on two completely different planets. My father had what people generally described as a "larger than life" personality. He was a small man and reminiscent of Anthony Quinn, whom he had met in Rome a few times. He knew that this was the impression he made on others. He was always on stage, always in the limelight, whether he was hosting a "searching for sunrise party" on his boat or had to have his diaper changed four times a day in an intensive care ward in San Diego after an emergency operation on his colon. Shortly after his death, my mother, who did not get on well with him and still lives in the house where I had my first experience of snow, said something about him that was very harsh but apt: "The man was an exorbitant optimist."

He had every reason to be one. At the age of thirty-four, he became chairman of the administrative board of a conglomerate that mined iron and semi-precious stones and was involved in constructing the railways in Brazil. Ten years later he was the owner of a public debt fund on the Dutch Antilles with a special focus on South America. After that he had majority shares in a British trading company that specialized in importing African agricultural products, but he spent more and more time on his sailing boat in California and with some of the artists there. He had a pretty close friendship with John Baldessari.

I owe it to his brazen character that I took over the family business at an early age. One day he asked me to join him on his boat that was anchored in Plymouth Cove on Tobago—I had just begun my doctorate at Yale after completing a degree at Cambridge—where he disclosed that I should take over his company's trading business in London. I had already discovered after a few weeks in New Haven that academic life as a mathematician was not for me, particularly not in Connecticut. While he was sorting out tarpon bait on the foredeck of his sailing boat, he explained to me what he believed was important about the company. He did not have a great deal of new things to say. I naturally knew that the business had been involved for some years in the trading and cultivation of coffee, rice, and oil in southern and central Africa. He had especially big plans with new plantations in Sierra Leone and Liberia, which I was now to bring to fruition "on his behalf," as he put it.

Fourteen years have gone by and I have lived in nine different countries on three continents since then. While commuting between London, Hong Kong, and Phnom Penh, I met Betty at the house of a friend who was working at Hong Kong University at the time. Her father had been a British officer and her mother was one of the best-known Cantonese opera singers in the seventies. Betty taught comparative literature and focused on the development of narrative in novels from former British colonies. I hit upon the absurd idea of asking Betty for Cantonese lessons.

I enjoyed life in Asia at the time, particularly in Hong Kong. But I liked Betty even more. I did not need many language lessons to discover that.

Nevertheless, after the birth of our son Carlo we moved to London. Although I had spent part of my youth there, I was completely helpless at the beginning. Anybody arriving in the city as a newcomer initially discovered huge demand, rising prices, and endless waiting lists. You seemed to need an agent for everything: to find a reasonable flat, a mortgage-friendly bank, a school, or a family doctor. The property in Chelsea was more expensive than on Hong Kong Island. Houses in Belgravia changed hands for many millions of pounds and the buyers wouldn't even put in an appearance. More than half the flats on our street seemed to have no one living in them. Their owners were usually from the cadres of the post-Soviet realm of the shades that otherwise lived in Palm Beach.

Finding a suitable primary school for Carlo was at least as complicated as transferring our office from London to Guernsey. It seemed as if half the world—or rather the demimonde—plus kin wanted to come to London. Established families had adopted the practice of registering their children at the traditional high schools straight after they were born. Carlo's classmates came from Turkmenistan, Albania, and Saudi Arabia, and already at the age of nine swapped hardcore pornos on their iPads.

Then the crises came and didn't let loose of the economy: the fall of Lehmann Brothers, the covert dollar war with the Chinese, the collapse of the euro. Then the austerity programs introduced by Western governments, mass unemployment, urban unrest. Unveiling the secrets of offshore hubs, charges leveled at capitalism. When the civil war started in Sierra Leone, we had to lay off one third of our employees. We were only able to pull through because of the provisions that we had through deferred taxes at our office on Guernsey.

The issue at that time was not just personal survival or maintaining jobs and saving the assets from previous generations, but the simple question of what standard of living I would be able to offer my boys one day. Only once did we spend our holidays together for more than a long weekend—on my father's boat, ludicrously enough. The short time that I was able to spend with the boys was almost completely devoted to doing their homework with them.

My father died at the peak of the Wall Street crisis. As if he didn't want anything more to do with this perverse world. I had panic attacks. This fear did not directly concern me, but my family, and also minor things like a lost credit card or a missed flight. In my mind, it is this fear that locks you into your parallel worlds, and that feeds your bad conscience. It grows the more you submit to it. We all know the stories of people who were unable to cope and started taking drugs or drinking or committed suicide. It's possible that I was close to slipping during my time in London. My dad's death probably saved me. In a certain sense, he died for me. When sitting next to his bed, often with his many friends who called in to say good-bye to him, I suddenly understood what was meant by the term "an accomplished life." He was not so old, but he had accomplished his life. He showed me what it meant to have arrived at the end, no matter who predetermined it. And that I still had a long way to go before arriving at that point.

I realized that we had to get away from London, away from the madness. We made the first arrangements to wind up the company a few days after a few close friends joined us to scatter my father's ashes from his boat into the sea off San Diego.

Karen 3

And another statement from the Manifesto of Frugal Innovation: "To ensure that Frugal Innovation can develop in real life, first the idea has to penetrate the minds of those whose needs it will satisfy in future. Before we can devote ourselves to the depopulated and neglected territories in our cities, we need to revitalize the conceptually void and neglected territories of our social awareness. Before we are capable of changing our situation, we must be able to interpret it.

"Our procedures, which have been refined and confirmed with the generous support of the island's Social Fund using surveys and public testing procedures, serve this purpose. New ideas can only be communicated in a new language, as illustrated by the example of the October Revolution and the popularization of the communist ideal in large parts of Europe more than one hundred years ago. The Russian revolutionaries discovered their eloquent ventriloquists in the avant-garde movement of the Constructivists.

"We are not thinking about the overthrow of society, but we need the same emphatic eloquence. Thus we are recruiting artists, designers, and hackers

97

for our mission. They are all researchers of a new language for a new generation; they are interpreters of a reality that needs to be redesigned. They are unified by the conviction that asceticism and frugality are the needs of the hour. That removing boundaries and political participation must become the goals of our actions. That action begins with us before it can take hold of others."

Padma 3

He had not told his employer, Mr. Xylouris, the whole truth. Sujit's life reads as if it were taken from the endless serial novel of Malayali men who have suffered a raw deal. He most likely lost his faith of settling down anywhere else before he arrived here. First, he tried to settle in Dubai. One quarter of all the men from Kerala have worked in the Gulf and even a few years ago had sent home many billions of dollars to their families. The Gulf was first a pot of gold for them and then later turned out, too late, to be a nightmare. The idea was to slave away for a few years and then enjoy the good life at home. That was how they imagined it. But sweating away at fifty degrees in the shade is more than sweating away—it is human torture. A Malayali with no training, no rights, no knowledge of the language, no face, no wife and child, is only a miserable shadow of a Malayali.

This shadow of the man came home one day. And what did he discover? He was not needed. He was not welcome. People had gotten used to his absence. He had become a stranger to his family, friends, and the village. He had always sent some money home and made it easier for them to live in the tropics. Now he was not contributing any more money and was living off of them.

That could have happened to Sujit too. But he was a clever person. At some stage, he could not bear life in the Gulf any longer. At night he'd lay on his plank bed in the work camp at Jebel Ali, unable to sleep, and finally recognized that he would not be happy either on this or the other side of the Indian Ocean. So he broke the spell of commuting between Dubai and Kerala and came here. He could have made it. He could have settled here, as many Malayalis or Goans have done during the last few years.

But Sujit did not want to abandon his coffee plantation in Ernakulam. Instead he wanted to leave his wife and children with the illusion that they could live a contented life in God's own country. That is what Kerala is to the Malayalis: God's own country. But God sends his men to hell as soon as they're ripe for it. Or he sends them to this island.

Karen 4

My last contributions documented the central statements of our strategy. Our pilot projects also have overall concepts. I'll describe a few of them now.

The first example is the mobile flaneur university. It was founded because of a deep-seated mistrust in committees of experts and political technocrats and the substantiated, energetic resulting demand of upholding the right to participation.

Francis Bacon's "Knowledge is power!" deserves to be reassessed in light of the politics of technocrat experts. We do not want to become experts, but we want to understand the results of their thinking. Just as we are only capable of applying scientific laws when we know their derivation, so can political positions be assessed only after their history is analyzed. Political knowledge needs to become knowable again!

There are now branches of our flaneur university in more than forty countries. Following on the tradition of traveling booksellers and their racks of books, our mobile libraries with reference books and electronic slide lectures roam through cities thirsty for new knowledge. Fitted with lightweight outdoor furniture in the blink of an eye, public squares serve as temporary sites for educational work. The library contains readers on the latest findings of Frugal Innovation. The lectures provide some basic knowledge of the relations between the economy, urbanism, and nonpartisan democracy. They embody our mission of interpreting reality and recognizing truth.

Haruko 3

Both here and abroad I hear a lot about the unacceptable working conditions of the numerous foreign construction workers. Or about new 1-percenters who have holed up on the island, according to some source or another. Or about Lavapolis not really being eco-friendly. Outside you are automatically viewed as a kind of complaints box. It is difficult not to become defensive. Even if many of the statements are not true, there is no reason to put a gloss on any situation. The island is a strange place. But that's precisely the reason to focus on it. The cities where I lived in the past were strange too—unjust, ugly, environmentally harmful.

The difference is that you never have the feeling here that situations are irreversible and carved in stone. Everybody accepts that they are living in a temporary society. Nobody would think of accepting the island as it is, or use it as a freezer where you deposit your future dreams and wishes. That was the rule for most of us in the outside world: freezing our dreams. But the freezer, in the meantime, has lost power.

Maybe it has something to do with the fact that people in Europe and Japan live in a society that has already experienced a lot and has grown old. Even the children are somehow born old and can't picture that there is much left for them to experience. As if time were "finished." The weight of many thousands of years are sunk here—in the ground, in the houses, in bodies, in brains. We crawl over the parched soil of our homeland and can't keep our heads up because of the mighty pull of gravitation.

Stascha 3

The streets of Raches, a shockingly sleepy fishing village at the foot of the lava belt, are so narrow that I twice missed the garage entrance to the rack railway to Point Alpha. Fortunately the ride only takes four minutes. I was surrounded by a family from my home country. The family had three boys who were wildly enthusiastic about everything that their childish eyes see. Lightly energized, the father pointed outside and speculated to his offspring how nice it would be to have a little house down there …

I must admit that I too am moved by the view from three hundred meters up. Two hundred and forty-six square kilometers are quite large. Admittedly not large enough for the prince's expansive enlightenment. He is even building out into sea and has for some time been spreading his wings in other countries. The critical visitor's gaze gets caught on Captain Kirk's stranded Super Twizy. Lavapolis will soon be experiencing expansion, according to the most popular article about the island—a "self-regulated urban organism," which will be linked to the main island only by suspension bridges. "Clean-tech city" is the urbanist's new primal scream. Maybe you shouldn't be an environmentalist if you want to stay alert in the face of such blandishments.

On the other side of the island, far enough away from the sublime residential world of Water City, extends Container City, the world's third-largest goods handling area. The colorful pyramids of thousands of steel containers look like a Legoland replica. Right next to it is the airport—its neon-green buildings look like a swarm of poisonous worms from here. By now more aircraft take off and land here than at any other Mediterranean destination. Last year fifty-two million people were transported here.

Figures like these encourage calculations: almost five square meters of the island per passenger, if all of them stayed. Actually most of them don't really disembark—they transfer to their next flight as they go from Asia to America, for example. Terminal Gamma handles the external immigration for the United States. Anybody who travels on to Atlanta or Chicago from Terminal Gamma uses an American domestic flight. Advance passport checks. There is no doubt that the

Chinese and Indians are delighted that the immigration laws are becoming increasingly tough around the globe.

So many people that visit a place just to travel on to somewhere else. A stream of fifty million passers-by on the island. The day after tomorrow I'm going on a tour of the Gray House. Of course I am excited. While princes elsewhere call their homes "Palace," here it is called "The Gray House." Again with this disguised arrogance. If I get the opportunity, I'll ask the patron how satisfying it is to watch the world passing by.

Karen 5

Escape Kitchen is a campaign of commemorative culture. At first sight their trolleys are hardly any different from normal snack bars. Cobbled together from transport bikes and travel chests, these flying kitchens, however, offer unusual menus. The repertoire of our gastro-artists includes both local dishes that are not prepared anywhere else, and dishes from countries where wars are being fought and where people have been expelled. We have recognized that imperialist fast-food chains are not the only ones responsible for the extinction of local cuisine. Political and economic crises are just as responsible for the fact that millions of people have been robbed of their elementary right to maintain their eating habits.

Escape Kitchen does not restrict itself to archiving and preparing rare, local, and international dishes, but it also collects anecdotes about the people who invented them in the past or introduced them to the country. The way to history is through the stomach. Escape Kitchen is a walking university, writing history down and telling it to curious customers. Our kitchen activists make their way through the streets of the cities. They do not restrict themselves to exotic snacks, but keep alive the memory of people who live or lived among us as the silent witnesses of their own displacement.

The Hanging Gardens of the Bats is an intervention to protect a species whose importance for the urban ecosystem is underestimated by many city dwellers. Bats are generally regarded as a plague. So the artists in our network have created an appropriate habitat for them: a mechanism with nest-like containers that easily stretches between two apartment buildings. Thousands of bats now live in the hanging garden landscapes that we have constructed in Mediterranean cities.

When we've better understood the way that our environment interconnects, we will go about changing it in our interest. Action follows interpretation. Many of our interventions serve to enrich public space. We believe that the neglect of public space is a clear sign of the decline of the social system. Neglected public space is the broken mirror of our society. We need to recapture this space in order to reinvigorate the exchange between human beings, which can only develop when protected from commercial terror.

Simone 5

The movement goes back to the mid-nineteenth century. Back then aristocrats and artists bade a sentimental farewell to each other in romantic alcoves. The first generation of libertine thinkers without any prospects of support from royalty was dismissed from this era into the next—which still didn't have any use for them.

The added value of critical art was not yet recognized by potential interested parties.

The response to not being needed was creative parasitism. Its adherents perhaps had a lively spirit and resilient talent, but the profession of a public intellectual could not be found in any trade directory. These people had nothing to sell but themselves. For a place to rest their head, they sold themselves to the powers that be, or even to their enemies. But a new system gradually emerged from the tangle of social strata, revolutions, fashions, techniques, and tempos in the mid-nineteenth century.

The following generations in this path of employment not only grew in number, but also in political and economic influence. You could no longer recognize that they came from families of parasites. Although there were always relapses—voluntary or involuntary retreats from the market—public intellectuals have continued to enjoy a great status in most societies since then.

In our own situation, we can see that this continuity is coming to an end. It's no longer possible to deny the disappearance of this profession; it can no longer be ignored that the familiar system of the market, which seemed to be indestructible, is heading toward self-destruction. Of course there are still vigilant and ruthless observers, and many schools continue to teach critical thinking, but the institutions that formed the base for the actions of this group are effectively as shattered as the market that they belong to.

Just like our forerunners more than one hundred and fifty years ago, we are being dismissed from an age without having any ready suggestions for the next one. Like them, we're momentarily superfluous and don't know whether we'll be needed in the future. Like them, we're making ends meet through creative parasitism that discovers its freedom in not having any obligations other than toward itself.

Padma 4

Although Mr. Xylouris later made great efforts to suppress his bad conscience and treat Sujit as he had before his India trip, it was obvious to the two men that something fundamental had changed between them. His foreman's work performance declined and his employer's dissatisfaction grew. Sujit disappeared almost a year after Mr. Xylouris had visited him. We paid out the insurance premiums from the fund to his family, but never received any response from them. I found out through my sister, who lives at my parents' house, that Sujit left his wife and children. They suspect he is in the Gulf, in Qatar or Abu Dhabi, on one of those voracious building sites. Back in hell, at any rate.

The idea of leaving home and moving to another country is still new to most people. Even if modern life enables them or even forces them to change their partners, jobs, flats, they usually stay citizens of the country where they were born. Even the Malayalis normally remain residents of Kerala on paper, although they leave the country right after becoming adults, like Sujit or me. They often live between two worlds, that of their parents and that of their employers, and cannot decide which is better. They do not even have the chance to decide. Neither the first nor the second offers a life that is desirable or one that they would choose for themselves. So Malayalis like Sujit do not just remain foreigners, they are estranged. Being estranged is worse than being a foreigner. They may even have a family, a house, a piece of land, and yet they are suspended midair and can't find a foothold. These people do not find their place in the world because they are torn between different locations and duties. The circle often only closes for people like Sujit when they've lost everything.

Simone 6

The author of *Le spleen de Paris* is one of my ancestors. He moves through the dawn of the capitalist world with a vigilant, merciless look and a nervous nose for the scent for impending fragmentation. He immerses this look within the darkness of misery and the glamour of early bourgeois splendor. The weary eyes of the poor emerge from the darkness. Their listless astonishment crosses the invisible threshold of light. The light is appalled and demands them to be banished to the darkness. The poet discovers his reflection in the semidarkness. He does not disclose the direction that he will take. His mad hatred and his frantic curiosity do not provide any clues.

I move through the dusk of that poet's world. I have followed him for a long time with my eyes open. But now I abandon him. I know where I belong. My pathway takes me back into the dark. I sense the eyes of the poor—no longer listless, in a shimmer of light. Later I'll talk about the arrival of this light.

Dasha 3

They call me Strelka at the office. I was running all over the place during my first few months, as if I'd misplaced my handbag. But I just wanted to organize our new life as quickly as possible. My boss asked me at some point what the Russian word for "arrow" is. "Well, *strelka*," I replied. That's how I got my nickname. Because I shot through the office like an arrow.

That settled down as time went by. But my nickname stuck, without anybody thinking much about it—apart from me. I later realized that the dog that was shot into space a while ago on a test mission was also called Strelka. In the Soviet Union, which used to be my home. It was not the first dog in space, but the first one to return alive. Perhaps Strelka survived because she didn't fly alone. There was a second dog, Belka, in the metal capsule, the Sputnik. There was also a rabbit, mice, rats, and who knows what else. The Sputnik was a real Strelka's ark …

Maybe that fits my nickname; maybe I'm also a test dog. But I was the one doing the launching. The first expedition was to Israel, the second to Austria, the third here. In each of these countries I worked for a public office that was supposed to make life easier for foreigners in their new surroundings—an environment as strange to me as it was to them. Most of my protégés naturally came from the Soviet Union. I benefited from the fact that I grew up speaking Hebrew and also studied German. And my fellow countrymen are usually clueless about foreign languages.

Nowadays my protégés come from all over. I mean it seriously when I call them protégés. Actually they deserve my nickname too: they've set off into what is an unknown world for them. Some of them arrived here in something like a metal capsule, in a shipping container or a rusty motorized sloop. They are all Strelkas. But they are called the Yellows here. Not because of the color of their skin, but because in the fifties and sixties immigrants received an ID card made of yellow cardboard.

Strictly speaking we'd all be among the Yellows, since one hundred years ago the island was still deserted. But now this term only refers to illegal immigrants—people who live here without a residence permit, permanently or temporarily.

The Transient or Temporary Yellows are a group that keeps to themselves. They are usually younger people from Europe or other Western countries, who to all appearances arrive with a tourist visa but set up their base here and commute between the island and the mainland. Many of them come from middle-class families, even if the middle-class isn't in such good shape. As long as they don't work illegally, don't get involved in criminal activities or become dependent on social security, the authorities are unlikely to check them.

I mainly work with the Permanent Yellows. A few weeks ago I sent a memo to the manager's office to say that they should reconsider using the description "Permanent Yellows." After all, hardly anybody is illegal their whole life, at least not here. They assured me that they would consider the matter.

The Permanent Yellows are usually less mobile than the temporary ones—less flexible and adaptable. Many of them are abroad for the first time and come from very poor backgrounds and hardly speak a word of English. Many are Muslim. It is the same as everywhere. Somebody manages to reach the country with the help of a smuggling ring, for example, or through friends or relatives. Or they try to arrive at night over water—although the chances of succeeding now are very low. Later they arrange for their relatives to join them. In some cases that involves a few dozen souls from four generations. Sooner or later the authorities catch up with them—something about the registration for their children at school or for a residence permit is not quite right. Or they are caught working illegally—unfortunately some people still do that here. Or they are caught by a patrol. The classic example is the identity check at one of the three public phone booths in Lavapolis. Why should you need to use a public phone booth, unless you're here illegally!

I can just imagine these people's fear—of the police, of people knocking at their door, of neighbors' looks. We were afraid all the time in the Soviet Union—of the police, the neighbors, the doorbell. But people here tend to be supportive. Rarely do they go to the police. There is no compulsion to get mixed into other people's business or denounce them. That is the subtle difference between my old dreary home and here. On the contrary: illegal immigrants often find a local resident who will rent a flat for them or register their children at school. But everybody knows this isn't a long-term solution.

As in other countries, illegal immigrants have to subject themselves to a process of legalization. Of course the probability of being allowed to stay here is higher than almost anywhere else in the world. Our population is supposed to grow by 5 percent each year and the job market is growing in line with this. But it is not just a question of being willing to work. The criteria of performance and need are formulated in a generous manner. The migration policy assumes the principle that there is a place in society for every person who obeys the law. Here they call it the principle of universal solidarity.

So you just need to recognize the rules that apply on the island—and obey them. No wonder that people from Arab countries struggle with the integration process and that the number of deportations among them is above average.

Our department's job is to prepare the Yellows undergoing this process for their test. Professional skills, physical condition, and the competence that we call universal solidarity are all tested. My colleagues are technical instructors and social workers who prepare the candidates by working through specific everyday situations with them. In these scenarios applicants are challenged to view their previous political or ethical attitudes from a new perspective—the new perspective being that of the island. At the end of each session there should be an insight. For example, you raise your children, but they don't belong to you. You can be a citizen of several countries, but you need to commit if there's an emergency—you are not allowed to do military service in another country. Or: there are no unbelievers, just people who believe different things. Or: if you're earning more money than you're spending, you must invest part of it in the country. Or: money is not equated with happiness or power.

I have taken it on myself to provide the candidates with some national history. Many of them do not even know the port at Lavapolis or Mount Bouno. They have never heard of Prince Theodore. We also watch films at the Universal Agora of people who have settled on the island talking about where they come from and how they arrived here. The applicants also have to pass a simple English course so that they can get along in public. That is sometimes the biggest hurdle. But each of them gets a chance. About 70 percent of the Yellows pass the test. This, of course, is just the start of the adventure for many of them. The future is always different from what we imagine—or as it appears in the films at the Agora.

Sometimes I think that you can't shake off your Strelka fate. Once a Strelka, always a Strelka. Always moving in dark outer space, in a more or less comfortable metal capsule. The island, for the Strelkas who land here, is outer space. Those who are here long enough and keep their eyes open realize that the island is not as small as it seems. It's changing all the time! Nobody does the same job here or lives in the same flat all their lives. Colleagues, neighbors, job prospects, the way of the road—nothing stays the same forever. Arriving here is not a real landing. The journey continues. We're not living in the future. We're living *before* the future, where it's just beginning. You have to watch out for loneliness. Still, this isn't a bad place for a Strelka.

Fabio 4

There has recently been a lot of talk about class struggle and suppression. Communism is suddenly an option that people are taking seriously again. Its opponents naturally deny the concept of social classes. I am hardly suspected of being a communist. In my opinion, classes definitely exist. There's a huge chasm between bankers and industrial entrepreneurs. I never liked people who are only busy with money. One of my professors at Cambridge once explained to me where the arrogance of the financial sector has its historical roots: in British large-scale property ownership. In the early nineteenth century the English nobility rather quickly discovered the benefits of industrialization. It turned out to be a perfect tool to become even richer without considerable expenditure. The string-pullers in London provided the new class of factory owners with money and land. They needed both to set up their production facilities. Industry increased the money of its creditors without the nobility or the city having to get their hands dirty. They preferred to leave that to the wealthy industrial upstarts and looked down on them with disdain. So from the start there were two types of beneficiaries in the emerging era: the so-called gentlemen capitalists and the factory owners.

Money owners have been far more powerful than owners of goods for a long time. In the goods/money relationship, there is a certain balance between the purchaser and the vendor. In purely monetary terms, on the other hand, the purchaser always has to adopt the role of the beggar and the vendor behaves like a demigod.

The fetish for money is a well-known phenomenon. Which doesn't make it any less exasperating. And it appears at the moment as if the magic of money is not inexhaustible. There are definitely people who say that it is easier to imagine the end of the world than the end of capitalism. But perhaps these people are wrong. The turbulence on the currency markets during the last few years illustrates that the power of the monetary capitalist may possibly be limited. The monopoly of governments to print money no longer seems to be as attractive since the belief in currency security has disappeared. The value of paper money could be reduced to its fuel value one day, as in the days of excessive inflation almost one hundred years ago.

This is possibly just speculation. My natural aversion to the arrogance of bankers and financial wizards certainly plays a role here. At any rate, shortly after my arrival on the island, I started to become involved in a network that is dedicated to spreading an alternative currency and combating the power of classic money, along with its lords and its markets. The network operates in a fully decentralized way and does not use any trustees. No government or bank can destroy it. It has introduced a currency for a type of goods exchange that no longer recognizes the monopoly of banks and money printers.

The first units were only worth a few dollars until recently. Suddenly the exchange rate rose to over fifty, then to two hundred, and finally to four hundred US dollars. There are now twelve million virtual units in circulation with a value of almost five billion. What happened?

I think the mistrust of many people is directed against two players in this unpopular system: the state and the bankers. Conditions that were long accepted, albeit reluctantly, are now being questioned. But this is not just a protest. The pressure is simply forcing people to become creative and to experiment—with their lives, their work, their future. Money is part of this experiment.

As I said before, it is my impression that this does not just involve mere resistance; it certainly doesn't involve destruction. This results sometimes in quite reasonable alternatives. The website of the network that I'm engaged in is not only operated anonymously, but the units are also issued according to an algorithm that has been set permanently. Circulation is already declining. So there won't be an uncontrollable bubble.

But the project can only be successful in the long term if its currency creates trust—stable trust. Its purchasers must be able to assume that there is an equivalent value to this new money and that this value will still be available in a few years' time. Among other things, my company has helped to ensure that you can purchase almost anything with this currency: from a diving holiday on the Maldives to stock shares or health insurance. It only worked in one direction for a long time: people bought the virtual units by bank transfer, kept them in an Internet piggy bank, and used them for online shopping if they were accepted. The currency area was therefore restricted to the product markets where they worked as the means of payment.

Exchanging traditional currencies for virtual ones is no longer a one-way street. This is exactly what we've made sure of. We operate along the lines of online exchange offices where our units can be traded into all major currencies. The classic money markets finally accepted the units, giving them the breakthrough into the financial world. We launched a hedge fund last year—the securities were sold three weeks later and have since risen in value.

Our network has been compared to Madoff or the tax-evasion mafia. Others believe that virtual currencies are the money of the future and the end of national states. Both views are certainly exaggerated. But our units are now worth eighty times more than when they were introduced a few years ago. Their number will remain restricted, so inflation is unlikely. Their real career began when banks in our neighboring countries became insolvent and investors were looking for an alternative to the unpopular euro. The sense of distrust in state currencies will increase in the near future.

I would have merely changed sides and joined my enemies, the monetary capitalists, if my intention in becoming involved in this currency network had simply been to make a few people rich on the Internet and serve my own needs along the way. But my interest lies in breaking the monopoly of private and state banks with alternative currencies. We wouldn't accomplish this by just creating a few major assets. A monetary system that could be taken seriously should not, in my view, primarily cause people to stockpile money, but it should make the exchange of goods and services easier and therefore enhance the whole economy. It looks as if this can only be achieved if monetary capitalism has a serious rival.

Friday 3

Streets and squares have become a lawless hunting ground. The alleys of Bari have long belonged to criminal gangs from Albania and Apulia. The Internet is gradually becoming a battle zone as well. Physical and virtual public space is a breeding ground for criminals. This led to our group on the island joining forces with the Frugalists and graffiti artists. We now form a united front against criminals in the public realm. This united front of socially committed hackers and graffiti artists is battling commercialism, gentrification, pauperization, social exclusion, restrictions on the use of software, surveillance, and environmental pollution. We favor total transparency, a borderless Internet, an inclusive society.

Graffiti is our language; the digital code, our alphabet. We follow the messages of cryptograms. Our projects oscillate between the physical and the virtual realm. They decipher the nightly soliloquies of the cities and transform them into infinite data streams. The subway is our broadband; the screen, the asphalt where we fight our battle. This united front thrives through networking with many all over the globe. *Release early, release often.* Share your knowledge, your art, your fun, and share yourself too. The hackers and graffiti writers of the world have united. They will reclaim the public domain as freedom from commerce and freedom of expression.

Friday 4

We support free software. Freedom for users to implement, copy, distribute, analyze, change, and improve intellectual property! Intellectual property is there to be distributed, improved, and adopted. The network is the owner of intellectual property rights and is constantly growing and spreading. We do not recognize individual property. Individual property enslaves people and is a tool of suppression. Individual property suppresses itself, because it prevents property from being distributed freely and improved. We exclusively recognize intellectual property that belongs to the community. The community of users is free and shows solidarity with its knowledge, its ideas, its art, its fun. Nothing belongs to the individual. Everything belongs to everybody.

We are combating all forms of undesirable distribution of marketing and propaganda. Protective filters developed by our hackers prevent the transmission of information that is of no interest to the recipient. These filters offer menus that can deactivate or misdirect user-hostile cookies. Even websites with relevant and user-friendly information for the public cannot escape the filth of commercial and invasive content. Our filters enable us to block out this kind of content. Internet users must be free to decide what information they wish to receive on websites and what they do not want. The protective filter menus are free software and are used in flexible ways. In emergencies, the menus can perform operations that not only detect and prevent the gathering of user information, but also disrupt and push back the service provider.

Friday 5

The emergence of the Internet has meant that virtual relationships have replaced real ones. In the end, people living on the same floor of an apartment building had nothing more to say to each other, but they came alive in a community scattered across half the planet. At some stage, public life withdrew from the streets and squares and moved to the Internet. This also had its advantages. The facade of an apparently vital urban society, which our cities have maintained for a long time, blocked our predecessors' view of a growing turmoil and the creation of a shapeless and uncritical mass. We are no longer looking through the alley for the face in the lively crowd (like Engels and Poe). The alley does not show any faces anymore. It's not even an alley anymore, but an element in the fractal landscape made of concrete and electric pulses, which is inhabited by the masses. We see the threads that run through this space. We follow these threads and come across vigilant communities once dominated by the boredom of the lonely consumer or of nothingness.

Friday 6

We view many rules in the real legal world as unjust. But we do not intend to break the rules in the real legal world. We break the rules in our minds and in the minds of those who join us. This freedom enables solidarity to grow. We also use it to create a vivid idea of the opportunities that would be available if we broke the rules in the real legal world.

Friday 7

We welcome the distribution of confidential information that was used to suppress free individuality. The state eavesdrops on its citizens and industry sniffs out its customers. They talk about security and mean betrayal. Citizens and customers have tolerated this for long enough. Now that the bare and rotten facts about total spying have been revealed, what Benjamin Franklin once said is clear: They who sell their freedom for a little security deserve neither one nor the other.

Simone 7

The early nineteenth century equipped the public squares in its cities with circular panoramas—monstrous wall paintings, some of them fifteen meters high and one hundred meters long—with the aim of providing as natural a picture of idyllic landscapes as possible. This illusionist genre of painting was later interpreted as the triumph of the city over the countryside, or more generally of art over nature. Because city dwellers integrated the natural landscape into the urban arena, they proved their cultural superiority over the countryfolk.

The early twenty-first century equips its cities' public squares with billboards that display graphic representations of building projects. The style is the very opposite of lifelike—it is hyper-artificial. This illusionist art celebrates a different triumph: the triumph of engineers and investors over time. They project a vision of what has not yet been built in the urban arena. These renderings show a picture of the near future that is already being created. They offer glimpses of the future and show that their clients support growth and technical progress.

Renderings develop their clout in various stages. Architects use them as the first part of their communications repertoire. Their artistically concealed perfection, anticipating the future, helps manipulate the imagination of potential providers of capital. Once the deal has been sealed, the renderings start to have their public effect. They are set up at the gates of a building site and are then supposed to manipulate the imagination of the urban community. The citizens are the potential customers of tomorrow. Renderings sell the future. Anybody who can sell the future is its master. The secret message of renderings communicates a power that is particularly desirable in the twenty-first century: power over time.

The global crisis has granted the renderings a third phase of effect: that of a heterotopia. Many building sites are temporarily or permanently closed, but the billboards with the promises of projects geared toward the future still stand there. They now speak of a future that, in all economic probability, will no longer occur. Their improbability invites the urban community to dream about what might have been if things had gone differently. The renderings then become panoramas of a fictitious world.

This connects architects with the scenographers of science-fiction films. The sets in film utopias (and dystopias) often remind people of architects' renderings—and vice versa. A whole software industry has risen that makes use of these heterotopian future productions using futuristic architecture and its artificial atmosphere. It is just this slightly alienated level of reality that convinces everyone that the future certainly won't look this way.

In the second half of the nineteenth century, the spectacular circular panoramas were superseded by photography. Photography heralded a new level of realism. This also applied to the way city dwellers viewed themselves. Their poorest members were the first to enjoy the bitter, sooty aftertaste of the triumph that the city had celebrated over the countryside decades before.

The third phase of the architectural renderings, along with the entire trompe l'oeil production of the early twenty-first century, is starting to give way to a new anti-triumphalist realism. Its color is gray, its message is frugality, and its platform is this island. While architects' future promises fade as sad works of fiction on billboards in the outside world, the principality's settlement policy is returning to the old wisdom that the city is the place of its residents, not of its houses.

Haruko 4

I sometimes travel for Goodshare. I hardly ever need the ferry to renew my passport stamp. There's an extremely wide network of links between the island and the outside world and it's easy to quickly land right in the middle of it. It turns out that Lisa's group may have its center here, but it mainly operates abroad. It's not really surprising. The outside world is both exorbitantly poor and exorbitantly rich. Many of the poor are, in turn, exorbitantly rich in ideas. We—organizations like Goodshare—help them to discover their riches. What's more, Goodshare constantly continues to learn through contact with new exchange initiatives and then distributes this new knowledge.

In abstract terms, the island is a platform that launches ideas that emerge somewhere in the world—in a city besieged by misery, or in the well-heeled home of a nerd on the island, or on the Internet. My own work is a good example of this. As I've already reported, this is the first time I'm doing a job where I actually use what I studied at university. Common House was just the beginning. With Goodshare's help I'm spending more and more time on other islands or on the Mediterranean mainland. The needs are there—we have the resources here to at least meet some of them. One of our latest projects is called Day Labor Station. It was suggested to us by an aid organization that was set up in the overgrown suburbs of Athens. Day Labor Station is a service for just that, day labor—there are half a million day laborers in the whole region. They hang around on public squares and offer their working skills for sale. They are often the target of a social rage that really should be directed at the top 1 percent—but those are well barricaded. So we set up facilities that look like bus stops and are equipped with toilets. Day laborers can find shelter here from bad weather and aggression. We have now set up these Day Labor Stations in fourteen Mediterranean cities in Europe.

The merchant who provided the aluminum frames for the roof coverings, which he'd dismantled elsewhere, earned his money from the project. The team at the Day Labor Station is a mix of headstrong pros, including two junkies, who work voluntarily just like us. I'm the architect in the group and designed the stations. The junkies were my advisers. They always looked at the drawings first and would find fault with one thing or another, which I'd then usually change.

I'm really glad to have junkies as experts. Architects are always expected to find solutions—so they deliver solutions. But they often don't even know the problems they're supposed to solve. But those architects who pose questions, or don't identify with this claimed sense of purpose, don't get a chance at all. Either you meet all the wishes of your client, who's often a megalomaniac, or you go out of business. That's the rule of international architecture competitions. Fortunately, projects like Day Labor Station take place without any public tender.

Fabio 5

My father was particularly proud of his collection of landscape marble. We display them now as they were displayed before—in glass cabinets made of cherrywood and cut glass, which I set up in a separate room in our flat. He apparently found the largest item in the collection himself near Congonhas, not far from our home at the time. The polished surface of this stone looks remarkably like a mountain landscape with green hills, a white church on top, and a flock of gray-feathered birds flying with outstretched wings toward the faint light on the horizon. I often looked at this stone as a child. I thought that it must've been made by an artist. Dad then explained to me that nature was the greatest artist of all, and this stone was one of its masterpieces.

The collection has now aroused my sons' interest. In contrast to me, they would never think that these stones were works of art. Their eye is trained for graphic perfection. What humans make, in their opinion, must not deviate from this perfection. We might complain that computer technology is oversaturating youthful imagination. But when is imagination oversaturated?

Perhaps computers have a very different effect, and I am experiencing this through the boys and how they deal with the collection. Because their eyes are technically trained, they immediately recognize the difference in a work of nature. Our boys are interested in these stones precisely because human hands did not make them.

Marcio came across a very surprising observation. He discovered a few weeks ago that the Congonhas stone has the same outline as the island. Since then, I've sometimes taken the stone out of the cabinet and imagined how it has accompanied me from place to place throughout my life, sometimes from a distance as well, from my childhood in Minas Gerais to here on the island. Like a sign that I've stayed on the right track. And that I've arrived where I was meant to arrive.

Haruko 5

Haruko means flower child. It's a common name in Japan and does not mean that my parents tripped on LSD or walked around in Jesus sandals. When those kinds of things were popular, they were still just school-kids. My mother was apparently thinking of Empress Shoken, whose real name was Haruko. She was the first empress who played a public role. Her unconventional lifestyle inspired Japanese women for many generations. But Shoken did not have any children. I've never asked my mother if she actually wants grandchildren.

As an architect, perhaps I really am a flower child. Or to put it more precisely, a designer who views her job in life as bringing people and the environment together. At university, as far as I understood artists and architects broke away from the convictions of their predecessors about one hundred years ago and moved their disciplines into a totally new direction. These people adopted the view that it was time to finally liberate humanity from the constraints that nature had placed on them. And this required an exclusively designed world that either barred everything non-human or submitted it to its own functions. This resulted in the anthropocentric house as the artificial contrast to untamed nature. In my opinion, the architecture that follows this line of thought often looks like a challenge to laws—those of stasis, climate, or light, for example. Or like a triumph over physical circumstances.

We now know that this architecture was a crackpot illusion. Human beings have locked themselves out and voluntarily moved into a cage. They now sit under a lonely sky and wait for somebody to finally come and visit them.

Simone 8
The journey through the fractal landscape of the present may be exhilarating, just as feverish strolls through the gas-lantern city intoxicated flaneurs in the past. The travelogues of the journeys are chaotic, full of fantasy and inconsistency. This in particular illustrates the poignancy of their observations and distinguishes them.

Haruko 6
Our houses can't withstand normal weather conditions, earthquakes, or floods. We are no stronger than nature and we cannot isolate ourselves from it either. If we do

not want to destroy it and ourselves too in the process, we need to see ourselves as part of it again, even if we interfere with it and change it. This paradox of an actor who acts within the system and whose initiative is directed at himself led me to the designs of fold architecture, which I have tried out in some projects in Lavapolis.

I started with the idea that geometry no longer provides a figurative order, but rather it provides an algorithmic method to interweave the orders of people, nature, space, and time. This geometry does not create definitive structures that exclusively serve people for their living or work, but rather it creates an organism whose functions change through the influence of nature in time. The spaces produced in this way begin to breathe, to ferment, and to die. They have their own life cycles and seasons. You might say that they are just as much living creatures as those who live in them. This produces an architecture of organic inclusivity. The resident returns to the space-time relativity of nature.

My employer is a development agency of the Social Fund, as was the case with Common House. I first designed a gallery in order to try out this new form of organic geometry. Instead of stringing together functions or piling them on top of each other, I folded an open surface in such a way that a topographic landscape was created with a gallery, a café, and a housing unit. The object looks like a mound of foam. Bubbles enlarge the surface area; the gallery looks like a natural labyrinth.

During the second stage we used the principle of surface folding on a whole house and developed a kind of habitable tree. The individual rooms are loosely layered on top of each other so that gaps form. These gaps are covered with greenery. Nature neighbors humans. Boundaries disappear through the inversion of interior and exterior, public and private.

The Social Fund liked the designs. We finally designed some building units in line with the geometric model of interweaving. The residential elements spread out in every direction according to the surface-folding algorithm. More tree houses will be created around the first tree house during the next two years and form the habitat for an urban tree nursery. We are returning to the point that the architects of the anthropocentric era, one hundred years ago, started off from, but in the opposite direction.

Stascha 4

That morning I really only wanted to look around Container City. Not, of course, in order to count the colorful stacks of metal containers. I am not a logistics expert and am more interested in people—the working conditions of low-wage laborers, for example. It was hard to squeeze any information out of the engineer who took me around. I was told that they have regular breaks, work comes to a halt if the temperature reaches forty-two degrees in the shade, the shifts last eight and a half hours, meal times are coordinated with the union representatives. He also introduced me to one of them—a small, pudgy bald guy in his mid-fifties with a strong handshake. He was Turkish. *On the Waterfront* immediately came to mind.

People here wear the popular yellow overalls and helmets. It's almost impossible to see them underneath it all—like armor, also to protect them against unwanted curiosity. But I still asked a few questions. One of them took me to his locker and showed me a photo of his girlfriend. He last saw her eighteen months ago. He said he wanted to travel home for two weeks in the summer. Home is not far away—Lamia, a city north of Athens. He told me that most people here are Greek. Then he looked at me. He wanted to know why I spoke his language—was I Greek? He laughed. He glanced at my blond hair and asked, "London?" "Sometimes," I told him, "but actually I'm from Skopje." He gave an absentminded nod, then his head shot up: "So you're practically Greek!" He shook my hand and called his mates over. I had trouble stopping them from pouring a drink for me from their thermos. The smell signaled it as ouzo.

They don't have it so bad here, I thought. And then one of my actual fellow countrymen turned up. More precisely, he jumped out of a crane cabin and rushed toward me. He yanked his helmet off—it looked as if his head was about to explode. Then he let me have it. I can still register his accent as coming from the East End of London. He said he had no time for assholes like me. We needed to make sure our own stuff at home gets straightened out again. The north has become a pile of crap, nothing more. And journalists were the flies buzzing all over it. Blowflies. He continued in this vein for some time. The engineer reappeared and tried to calm him down. "Forget it, Steve," he said. Steve wasn't paying any attention to him. Steve seemed untouchable, the way that he danced around between the others in front of his crane, spewing venom. Steve kept shouting,

"Criminal propaganda! You drag everything through shit! Especially if it's better than what you've got."

What hatred! The question was whether he hated or felt hated. The purple caricature of a crane operator's face. If it hadn't been so taxing, one really might have worried about his blood pressure. But each needed only to worry about himself at the moment. The man from East London—who sees his Mediterranean paradise threatened by a journalist from the outside world, as they call it here—pulled a wrench out of his trouser pocket and gave it a tentative swing in my direction. "Not here," Steve threatened. "Not here! The island is the last piece of land where you can still live a sensible life. Piss off, wanker!" he suggested. By now the saliva was running down his chin.

His shouting following me until I passed the dull clangs of a freight elevator hoisting a truck. The engineer gave me a wry look at the exit. He was happy when I shook his hand. Something was on his mind. He's probably from eastern Europe and was simply careful when speaking a foreign language. "Steve didn't mean it," he said. I tried to look sympathetic. "He's actually very sad, because of his son." My eyes followed a gull and I probably gave the impression that I wanted to get out of there. "Suicide," the engineer said. "Last week. In the city where you're from."

I strolled around the lava fields between the mountain pines for a while and held my face to the salty wind. A young woman was suddenly standing before me in a kind of canyon. She was directing a few workers who were busy working on the entrance to a hole in the rock. Apparently she had been expecting somebody and asked me with a sneer whether I was from the Social Fund. Disheveled and still preoccupied with Steve, I must have looked like somebody who'd lost his orientation.

But I had regained my curiosity. Accompanied by the workers, who seemed a bit amused by the fact that this young lady was wearing the same overalls as them, she led me into the hole and then stopped with a sense of expectation. She explained that this was her latest experiment in living and nodded energetically, as if awaiting immediate confirmation from me. The hole was actually pretty spacious, a kind of tuff cave with a dome-shaped main room, from which two tunnels, lying one upon the other, branched off. I kept a precautionary lookout for bats, but was quickly diverted by my guide. "Primitive Future House," she called out to me, and waved a laser pointer along the walls. In the LED glare of the mine lamps I gradually made out the wood and concrete trestles and the alcoves—from up close a structure like a nest of monster wasps. She maneuvered me through one of the two tunnels into a second area with similar fixtures. This space had natural light from above. I could now see that some of the alcoves had chairs and other furniture; there were even some pictures hanging on the walls. If I saw correctly in the semidarkness, they were manga comics.

She asked me to put on a helmet and announced that the access to the modules, as she called the alcoves, was a bit unusual. I crawled along on all fours behind her for five minutes, climbing through concrete crevices and over wooden slats. A bit like in *Caveman*. We then squeezed ourselves into one of the modules, which was barely one and a half meters high and felt more like a Finnish sauna. Fortunately there was a skylight here too. The woman offered me a kind of futon to sit on and held out a glass of water. She said that they didn't have coffee yet. I admitted that water would do just fine, and lifted the glass to my lips.

She had already launched into her lecture. The cave and the nest were two opposing primitive architectures, I was told. The nest was a design; the cave, a natural state. According to my host, future habitation will seek to harmonize both elements. An artificial cave—that's what she was testing out. I leaned back on the futon. I asked her whether she believed that people in future would live in caves again. She nodded as resolutely as before, adding that at least some people would. She believed that the flat of the future would not have any fixed spatial functions; it wouldn't even be just for living. It could be used as a storeroom, a foxhole, or a garden for nightshades. Or as a nest for large insects, I interjected.

She didn't seem to hear me. She was far too much in her element. She indicated that future habitation would not only involve humans. Animals, plants, and dead objects would have a right to a home as well. Humans would once again become part of a universal connectivity and soon wouldn't just observe the world from their point of view. The architecture of the future would be non-anthropocentric.

The woman was sitting on a mattress directly opposite me. If I had stretched out my hand, I could easily have stroked her cheek. If it hadn't been for her significant nodding every once and awhile, I would have congratulated her on a successful show. What she was telling me seemed rather rehearsed. And after all she had been expecting somebody else, presumably to bewitch him or her in the Primitive Future House with her new teachings on non-anthropocentric architecture. She even confirmed that she had applied for a grant for the project from the government.

I could only wish her well with this. But it didn't escape her notice that I wasn't really convinced, and this seemed to amuse her at least. She admitted that two years ago, she also thought that these ideas were mad. But she had lived in the outside world at that time too. The term "outside world" did not sound as contemptuous coming from her mouth as from Steve's. But it was sadder. She told me that her name means flower child. And that it was only here on the island where she'd learned to think positively about the future.

As I was making my way back to the Twizy through the lava fields, a tractor crossed my path. The driver flagged me down with his bony hand. His dark bald head glistened. A pair of bright, alert eyes regarded me. The man seemed to want to give me enough time to take him in. Then he asked me what time it was. I told him. He reminded me that I had to deduct one minute. I was able to astutely reply that I had already had. He opened his toothless mouth and said, "Well and good. Welcome to the system."

That's what I wanted to know more about. So he turned off the engine and put his hands in his lap. He asked me whether I knew why they had changed the time system. "Why?" I replied curiously. His eyes darted above my head for a moment as if they had discovered something unusual there. "Because of the need for creative destruction," he stated. He believed there wasn't any other reason. I must know the theory of the flat world—a world in which people could freely spread capital, services, and goods around the planet because there are no longer any borders to stop them. That's roughly what the driver said.

I admitted that I knew the theory. So he added that I needed to recognize that a boundless world would reach its limits at some stage. When all the people and goods and capital had been spread around the globe equally. It would be a kind of heat death for the global economy. I tried to reply with a friendly nod. He added that things were not as improbable as they sounded. He had clearly noted a hint of skepticism on my part. He asked me why the unemployment rate was so high, if not because of market saturation? And what about the population explosion? What about the last nature reserves that conservationists were trying to defend against human occupation and exploitation?

The driver was silent for a while to allow me to digest it all. "Only one thing is not expanding," he said, and winked at me. Time! It only exists for a moment, and then it's gone. Cooped up between the endless past and the endless present, standing quite still. For the tiny moment of its presence on Earth.

But if time stands still, how should it continue if the flat space available on our planet is first filled with human beings, capital, and goods? Wouldn't the world itself stand still then? The driver opened his mouth again as if to say something. This time it seemed as if he'd suddenly become terribly weary. We remained silent for a while and allowed the wind to blow. He asked me finally whether I understood where we were heading. I wasn't certain, I admitted. He said that time was the border of a flat world—that's what everything came down to! The old system of capitalism would be crushed as a result. There were already many signs of this.

He was rocking on his seat as if he could hardly wait to point out the signs to an ignorant person like me. He added that the island had had to destroy the limitation of time in order to keep the world going around in the future too. By isolating itself from the global time system, the island had created a new system of calculating time. Thanks to this system, new periods of time would automatically open up, and they would be occupied by people, capital, and goods again. The conquest had only just begun. We now needed to discover new worlds—and the outside world was just a grain of dust in comparison. A grain of dust! The driver now pulled a cap over his head and nodded in encouragement. "Welcome to the system!" he called back to me over his shoulder. "Those who want to create new spaces, first have to get rid of the old time system. The future lies in the minute!"

Simone 9

The social niche is the safe for the capital of the unborn.

During times of political totalitarianism, the niche was the cancer cell of the system. In times when the market is collapsing, it is the shelter for those who are not temporarily needed. Even Nietzsche knew that some people would be born posthumously.

Diamantis 2

Do not ask me why Kurios Theodore believed that I was the right man for the job. Until that point, money had never played a role in my life. I simply did not have any! The only houses I had built were the shed where I lived in Ikaria and the enrollment hut here. But I had to rebuild that three times. Nevertheless Kurios came upon the idea of giving me oversight of the strip. He stood in my hut one afternoon, as he had done a few years earlier in the vineyard, and said, "There's work to be done, come with me." As if there had not been any work to do up to that time. Such was Kurios—short on words and always preoccupied with the next job.

He then showed me the plans in his office. A week later an American turned up, James Desmarais. He was supposed to help me set up the administration—rather, the *management*, as we quickly learned to call it. After three months Desmarais had his fill of the mosquitoes and the heat, even though he came from Texas. He was replaced by two other people, who also left shortly afterward. When Keith Bower from Peersons started working, I had almost completely set up the administration on my own. But things progressed much faster with a company like Peersons on board.

For the next twenty-five years I didn't make it out of the administration. The strip was created under our leadership during this time. People came and brought money. Kurios was never satisfied, but he trusted me in everything. We both knew that we had managed to do something fantastic. But we never really got to enjoy it. I never even had time to fall in love with a woman. There were a few brief episodes. It was never enough to set up a family. So I kept working on the strip and when that was finished, I worked for the new airport. Even the initial plans for Container City were mine. The projects became larger and larger. Things had to happen faster each time. There was a lot of money at stake. It usually came from outside—and these people were always nervous.

When Kurios became ill, I realized that I had also become an old man. I had spent thirty-four years on the island. Of course the island had changed beyond recognition. And the same was true of me. But the island had become younger, spritely. I had played a part in this. I had invested my youth in the island. My whole life, really.

I was expecting to spend my final days somewhere else. I was naturally in Vegas a lot, so I tried to retire there after Kurios passed away. And the end did not seem that far off for me either. Eleven months after I had bought a flat in Boulder City with a view of the Veterans Memorial Park, I could hardly get out of bed each morning. It sometimes took me fifteen minutes to tie my shoelaces. The first doctor diagnosed an advanced stage of lung cancer and gave me nine months to live. I had certainly smoked enough during my life. The second doctor increased my life expectancy to three years, the third didn't want to name a figure, the fourth dropped down again to less than one year again—only after chemotherapy, of course, or perhaps an operation. I could have easily afforded that in the best hospital in Nevada.

You might think it mad, but one afternoon Kurios appeared on the balcony of my apartment. I was brooding over the cancer—which I did almost constantly at the time. He didn't say anything to me. He just stood there. I cannot even say with any certainty what he looked like or what he was wearing. He just stood there with his back to the Veterans Memorial and seemed to be looking over at me. He was not angry, just resolute.

I kept brooding over the cancer, naturally, but suddenly I knew that I couldn't die in a foreign land. I had to return to the island.

Outside Raches at Point Alpha I owned a small house, and there I waited for the end of my life, a second time. I hardly left the house during the first few weeks and was unable to take more than three steps without losing my breath. Iosif and Marius visited me from time to time. They were former colleagues from my time at the strip. Each of them was occupied with the last stage of life in his own way. They'd bring a bottle of red wine with them and we'd play dominos, as we'd done during our lunch breaks in the old days, until I'd fall asleep over the board.

I had never been particularly religious and was not especially worried about what would happen to me after I died. But I sometimes went over to the chapel, particularly because I thought I owed that to my neighbors and friends. There is a small vineyard next to the house. At first, I didn't have the strength to tend to it. But in the end, I started pottering around with it, as I had done on Ikaria forty years earlier. Once again I grew Kotsifali grapes.

After a few weeks I made a habit of buying fresh vegetables at the market each morning. Before noon

I'd also work in the vineyard without feeling faint or short of breath. Iosif and the other guys came fairly often. They brought more red wine and played dominos with me, until they would fall asleep over the board.

Perhaps you have an idea of where I'm heading. I am now 103 years old. Some of my friends still come to play dominos. Iosif is actually two years older than me. Nothing amazes me any longer. Kurios never came again; he only called me back here. I have simply forgotten to die.

III. In the Gray House

Stascha squeezes out of the Twizy. He stretches his back while examining the building in the copper light of the setting sun. Although it was only a ten-minute drive from the tennis courts in Novo Lavapolis, an unfamiliar feeling creeps through him. Rapture, he thinks. A holy sense of awe would be going too far, at least in his case. The feeling is caused by the curious appearance in front of him. The structure was like a physical continuation of the hill on which it was built. To the right and left, the sea glistened, like oil. Suddenly it strikes him: the volcano! As his plane was landing, Mount Bouno had also looked like this strange thing. A gray wrinkled cone. But here light penetrated from the creases.

People are emerging from their cars beside him and walking toward the cone in loose groups. He joins them without turning his eyes away from the building. Unlike Mount Bouno, the basalt walls have crevices. Narrow windows form irregular gaps in the facade. The deep, saturated lighting inside makes the cone glow. Like it is about to erupt. And yet Stascha thinks how tempting it is to lay a hand on its lined skin.

He picks up snippets of conversation from the crowd. He can't pick up the meaning; it's as if they're hinting at something that only they know about. As if they were headed to mass. He decides to behave exactly the same way: like an atheist in a church.

A man dressed in a gray suit is waiting at the entrance. With one hand in his trouser pocket and a faint smile he watches the people walk past him through the turnstile. It's Alberto, the director of the Department of Strategic Planning. Stascha has an appointment with him. They nod to each other, shake hands, and each gives the other a defensive wink.

"Welcome to the Gray House," Alberto says, and with a gesture of his hand invites his visitor to follow him inside the cone. "Since you don't just want to see the Agora, we'll go this way." While the other people step onto a steep escalator, the top of which couldn't be seen from the entrance, Alberto heads for a moving walkway, perpendicular to the escalator, leading into a tunnel. Complete silence envelops them now. The air is appreciably cooler than outside, absent the familiar drone of the air conditioner.

Alberto takes two pairs of tinted glasses out of a suit pocket, asks Stascha to put one on, and with his index finger pushes the other up the bridge of his nose. The tunnel was no longer a tube: it looked like a computer screen made of concentric rings. The light was so powerful that, despite the glasses, Stascha is forced to squint. But the further they go down the walkway, the more his eyes adjust and it becomes easier for him to make out the rings. What at first appeared to be a round screen of monochrome segments, turns out on closer inspection to be an elaborate play of transparent shadows and colors, which become stronger the further they walk down the tunnel.

At first Stascha imagines that he's seeing the outlines of a map on the screen, but the contours change again into something that looks like a multi-dimensional numerical graphic. Before he can decipher it, human bodies flit across his glasses, followed by schools of fish that suddenly change direction and turn out to be the text of some kind of encoded language. The images briefly emerge dimly from the rings of light, only to disappear again. Then the rings start to turn. Or was he turning? We must be close to the center, Stascha thinks, and clutches the handrail with sweaty palms.

"We're in the center," says a voice that's not his own. The rings of light disappear. Alberto takes off his glasses and winks at him. Stascha automatically does the same, inwardly amused by the sense of confusion that grips him. They were standing in front of a glass wall. On the other side, several dozen people, mostly elderly, were sitting in front of personal computers. Signs appeared on some screens like those Stascha thinks he just saw through the glasses.

"The Prediction Center, right?" Stascha says to his guide.

Alberto nods. "Part of the Department of Strategic Planning."

"Your colleagues there process big data and make forecasts. What primarily interests you here?"

"The basis of the data," Alberto responds. "Thanks to our citizens' cooperation in providing the data, we achieve a far greater degree of accuracy in real-time information than the outside world. Methods like real-time tracking help us to model potential events on our island in the near future, whether they're in the parliament, in everyday life, or off the coast."

"The people on the island hand over their complete private sphere and you use this, well, let's call it altruism, in order to adopt the most efficient corporate measures to control these people as much as possible. Is that what you mean?"

Alberto's wink seemed to suit any occasion. "You know that I don't have a mandate to conduct a debate with you. You can freely interpret everything you see and experience. I have a mandate to deliver as accurate a picture of reality on the island as possible. The center is not only a product, but the producer of this reality. We process the data that we handle here with the full knowledge of our citizens and in their interest. They're entitled at any time to reclaim the relevant information and process it themselves."

"The pictures earlier in the tunnel seemed like hocus-pocus to me."

"They're renderings that artists produce from our forecasts. Similar to the mock-ups of houses that have not yet been built. Only these renderings are used to simulate every conceivable political, economic, or cultural incident to come. The tunnel works like a reverse calculation of time. When we entered the tunnel, we first saw things that were very far off and thus appeared hazy. We then gradually approached the present. As a result, the images at the end of our journey became more and more concrete, for you as well. Experts from our department are able to read these renderings and draw conclusions for their strategic work. Any necessary changes to the law, adaptations of the budget, support programs—"

"Eavesdropping operations …"

"We're not in the bunker of a secret operation here. Our citizens have access to the database and are kept informed of the department's recommendations on the future through the Agora." Alberto crossed his hands behind his back, as if he wanted to make an important statement. "But before we visit the Agora, I would like to show you a specialty of our Prediction Center. We differ from the outside-world countries in many ways. This also applies to the Prediction Center. Of course, in our calculations we take into account all the available data that we can obtain from events in the outside world. For example, we're investigating to what extent the political or economic developments in countries in the outside world have consequences for us, whether other societies approximate our system in certain respects, and where new centers of conflict are emerging. We draw on this information—which, naturally, is incomplete—to predict developments in our principality."

"This simply sounds like spying for defense purposes."

Alberto removed his hands from behind his back and clasped them together in front of his heart. "Then let me try to correct your impression by pointing out," he drawled at a snail's pace, "that the processed data is confidentially made available to international organizations like the United Nations. A large number of our forecasts can be used in the outside world. But naturally only by institutes that use our information according to our charter of basic rights. As you know, transparency cannot be equated with open source."

It is warmer than it was in the tunnel. Stascha and Alberto are standing under a dome. Numerous concrete nests were attached to the dome's interior, all connected by a system of escalators and elevators.

Statscha thinks of the Primitive Future House. The space is bathed in warm orange-yellow light, but no lamps can be seen. He watches with fascination how visitors eagerly swarm to the nests via the escalators and elevators. "There's quite a lot going on here." His voice sounds unintentionally enthusiastic. Probably because his guide is enshrouded in silence ever since the two of them left the Prediction Center. "The Universal Agora is the real central point of the Gray House, and therefore of the island," Alberto replies and examines his counterpart inquisitively, as if looking for some unmistakable sign on Stascha's face to gauge how his explanation is being received. "In their spare time the citizens meet up here, surf through the collection or make entries in its archives. In the cities of ancient Greece the agora was the place where locals and outsiders met to do business or exchange news. It was, if you like, a shopping mall, TV station, and museum all in one: the origin of public space. We're standing right at the heart of the central public space of the principality, visited by committed citizens."

"Where's the prince?" Stascha asks, slyly. "Is he a committed citizen too?"

"Faidon has plenty to do, like everyone else. He's not here at the moment; he's in Container City."

Stascha peers at his guide through narrowed eyelids. "How do you know that?"

"Thanks to this instrument." Alberto takes a device that looks like a phone out of the inside pocket of his suit. "All citizens have a videopod like this one. They can, for instance, obtain information at any time about where Faidon is and what he's up to.

Faidon is—apart from a few private functions—an indispensable part of the Agora. He is, to a certain extent, its protagonist."

"Excluding any doubles?"

Stascha and Alberto exchange their practiced wink.

A young woman walks past them and gets onto an ascending escalator. She reminds Stascha of the woman in the cave. "What exactly are people doing here?"

"The Agora has various functions. Come with me."

They follow the young lady onto the escalator and soon enter one of the concrete nests. Stascha's eyes first have to grow accustomed to the environment with its dimmed lights. They have arrived in a screening room shaped like an oversized shoebox. There are six chairs opposite a terminal and a concave screen the size of a double door. Otherwise the room is empty. He dubiously sits down in one of the chairs. "This is one of our booths," Alberto's voice instructs from the semidarkness. "There are also booths that can accommodate up to fifty people. You can imagine the Agora as a museum, among other things, where the history of the island is told. We have a rich collection of objects from the few decades of renewed life on the island."

Alberto operates a few buttons on the terminal. The hologram of a three-mast sailing ship appears on the screen. The ship seems to move so that the observer can view it from different perspectives. The image moves closer; Stascha can now look into the ship's interior. He sees the bridge, the writing on a bronze plate above the steering wheel: *Attiki*. "The ship of the first disembarkation of Theodore Messinis," Alberto says, before his hands move swiftly over the keyboard again. "Here, the props of *Lido de Paris*, the first Vegas show on the island." Alberto zaps through a virtual collection of dance shoes, makeup cases, folding screens, and lace skirts. The face of a young man appears, then a small motorboat on a deserted beach. The boat is surrounded by clothes, plates, and food. "This is an example of how we document our latest history. Its dark side too. The young man was caught by the coastguard in this boat just a few weeks ago. He made his story available to the archives in the Agora." The man starts to talk: "Yesterday I stopped being one of the printless. I know that from our social trainer. The printless used to be the paperless ..."

Stascha made a few notes in the flickering light before the man finished his report. "What happened to him? Was he deported?" Alberto half turns at the terminal to look at him. He seems to be thinking. "I don't know. The decision will be made in three days' time. The appraisal of the center has been made available to the authority, but it cannot be accessed in a case that has not been completed."

"So there are limits to transparency?" Stascha shouts over to the shadow at the terminal. "How would you handle it?" comes the reply. "Give him a chance, if his story is true. Give him the opportunity to bring his family over too." A faint smile runs across Alberto's face, which does not escape Stascha. "Then you regard the principality as the better alternative for our candidates?"

They silently click through a series of documents that cover procedures in the late 1940s on the political legitimacy of Theodore Messinis and the diplomatic recognition of the principality by the United States. "You know," says Alberto suddenly, "for me, these files, documents, and items are not objects at all. They are subjects. They tell us a story that only they know. Ever since the Universal Agora has been in existence, I've understood what's meant by the fact that things are able to speak."

"I get it. But how talkative are your people?"

Alberto turns to his companion, crosses his arms, and leans back on the terminal. "You're right. The Biography Fund is the most important function of the Agora," he continues. "What you've seen from below, the dome, the booths, the people, isn't it like a replica of our life on the island? The dome represents the sky, and the booths, the housing. The Agora reconstructs every event that has taken place on its territory, every thought that has gone through the mind of each of its citizens—of course, only those thoughts that could be recorded in the archives with the consent of the citizen involved."

"Terrific. And how is this ... consent guaranteed?"

"I showed you the videopod earlier. Not only does it enable people to watch what Prince Faidon does every day. Our citizens can engage with the Agora through this instrument. From any terminal in the Agora you can contact any citizen over their videopod. If they accept the request, they automatically accept that the contact will be stored in the Agora's archives."

"That's what's called a social medium."

"I'm not saying that we've completely reinvented the wheel. But you must admit that the operators of social media primarily want to earn money. Our Agora, however, is protected from any commercial interests. Rather, it has two fundamental functions that paradigmatically reflect the heterotopian character of our social order. First of all, it represents an assessment tool for our Prediction Center. Citizens can participate in the political decision-making process through videopods. They have the opportunity to consider important public matters and assess and qualify them. You're familiar with this from other cooperation models perhaps, like consumer ratings on the Internet.

Secondly, the Agora is a collective art project. Depending on how actively a citizen is involved in the contact life at the Agora and how creative his or her contributions are, vivid and various exhibits emerge from life stories, and they can only be seen in these booths. Each person is involved in expanding the Biography Fund. This turns it into an artwork. We have, if you will, potentially six hundred thousand curators who are managing and enriching a collection of six hundred thousand human subjects. No more and no less. Compared to the normal social media, it's a village."

"Good. You have six hundred thousand curators. But who are the artists?"

"See, artists, curators, audience … there's no difference for us anymore. Everyone is an artist, curator, audience. Everyone tells stories and is also the subject of history. We have nothing against professional art.

It has its place in our archives too. Its creators belong to the community of the Agora like any other. But that's all. We don't share the conviction that artists might have more important things to say about us than others—than we do about ourselves, for example. They have *one* voice, that's all. What counts for us is the collective body, the citizens, their stories, their objects. We've reached one of the most important functions of the Universal Agora, Stascha. It liberates individuals from professional, material, religious, or other obligations to be either producer or consumer. It dissolves the contradiction between art and life. What you can see here is the island, both as fiction and as reality …!"

Alberto's fingers glide over the buttons at the terminal as if playing one of the last Beethoven sonatas. One after another, a woman of South Asian origin, a southern European in his forties with a work by John Baldessari hanging on the wall behind him, and a woman with a Slavic accent appear on the monitor. They begin to speak: "My dear mother gave birth to me in Aluva, Kerala … We became islanders—and we've never regretted it … Today marks the fifth anniversary of our arrival. Of course I can remember it like it was yesterday. It was dark when we left the airport …"

Alberto suddenly has his videopod in his hand. "Your Excellency, he'll be delighted," he half whispers into the device. He turns to the terminal again. "Prince Faidon will now answer your questions, Stascha," he calls over his shoulder to his guest. Stascha is not certain how much time he has spent in the booth. The head of a clean-shaven man of indeterminate age with olive-colored cheeks and close-cropped white hair appears on the monitor. A pair of glasses with a broad, angular frame magnified his slightly almond-shaped eyes. His turquoise irises stood out. The V-shaped neck of a black T-shirt formed the lower edge of the monitor screen. Alberto withdraws from the face back into the semidarkness behind the row of seats. Stascha sits with his right hand cupping his chin, like a bored spectator. But his counterpart looks at him from the screen with his blue-green eyes, unmoved and unspeaking.

"You're supposed to start!" Stascha hears Alberto urging him quietly from the back. A facetious grin covers his face.

"Good evening, Your Excellency!" he says to the screen. "Can you even see me in this dim light?"

"Good evening, Stascha. Of course. Welcome to the Agora. I'm looking forward to our conversation."

He has a relatively young voice, Stascha thinks, rather like a student's. Stascha then takes his hand from under his chin, runs it through his hair, and leans back. "Nobody has given me a time frame for this discussion. I will ask you a few questions that I've prepared. You certainly approve if I record them …"

As Faidon gives only a brief, friendly nod, Stascha pulls out his digital recorder from his pocket, switches it on, and puts it on the seat of the empty chair next to him so that he can keep an eye on the red light. He leans back again and starts in a demonstratively light-hearted tone, the corners of his eyes crinkling: "The island has, to put it politely, an unusual political history. Do you believe a monarchy is really a form of government that allows social progress, Prince Faidon?"

"Our history, first and foremost, Stascha, is short. This society has not had centuries to develop like Europe, China, or America. No great moments of glory have made us shine. In turn, no blood has been shed so far, and hopefully that will remain the case. We are, although quantitatively small, a product of unusual global history after 1945. When my father first set foot on this island, an empire of lava, sulfur, and ash had just come to its end after five hundred years. It's possible that Phoenicians, Vandals, or Turks may have gallivanted around here, but the volcano wiped out every trace of them. My father arrived on an island without any people and without any history. Virgin territory. His seizure of the land may appear like a primeval act, similar to the legally binding deeds of occupation that were normal in feudal times, when ruling over territory was the precondition for ruling over people. Autocracy was a necessary consequence of this, but also a temporary one. I'm sure that we're on the way to a new political system. We're working to do away with the principality."

"That sounds reassuring ... You've called the construct a heterotopia. But on closer inspection, it reveals itself as a tax haven safeguarded by US forces with a generous Social Fund. Where's the innovation here?"

"You're using terms like 'construct' and 'tax haven.' Perhaps you'll agree with me that one of the current basic evils involves disconnecting the financial markets from state and even from territorial dependences. Modern capital is dangerous because it is homeless. It comes and goes without taking into account the losses of others, as long as it can grow. The tax haven is now rather like a transformer. The money comes in with a certain voltage and leaves again with a different voltage. What's important is that it continues moving—at the speed of light, if possible. The oasis cannot detain it either. If you subject real tax havens to closer examination, you'll see that the general public in these kinds of exclaves doesn't enjoy a very high standard of living. Yes, there are rich people, but the public sector, apart from the police, is normally in a miserable state. Things are different here. We don't allow capital to slip in and out in an uncontrolled fashion. Instead, we offer it the opportunity of settling here under better conditions than in highly taxed countries. In return, we expect investments. We cause what was originally homeless capital to settle here. I'm certain the G8 finance ministers would like to do that in their home countries too. But the economy is at rock bottom, the social situation is tense, and they normally have nothing to offer volatile capital. If you've taken a close look at our island, you'll certainly have noticed that there are a large number of projects here that are managed by the public sector. They are education or subsidy programs, research, art. We can afford this because of the high inflow of finances. Many view this as an unnecessary luxury. Of course, we could use the money in some other way. But we're convinced that we need this luxury. Name one other tax haven where capital yields are used to promote business sectors that are inherently unproductive!"

"But there's still the security policy and your dependency on the United States."

"There are people who represent the view that

anybody who's not for us is against us. I view things differently. It's true that we were tied to the US in military terms for a long time. But since the withdrawal of their forces from our territory and the general recognition of the island in international law, our policy of neutrality has proved successful. We maintain direct and indirect political relations with most countries in the world and are one of the first signatories on many international agreements on security, environmental protection, and human rights. Our armed forces partly operate to protect our sovereign territory on the ground, on the water, in the air, and in cyberspace, but they also join in campaigns to fight terrorism, drug or human trafficking, and illegal fishing. Absolute independence is an illusion. Relative independence is, however, a foundation for life."

"You're surrounded by misery and twiddle your thumbs …"

"I'm grateful that you've given me the opportunity to explain our position. The island is well known for its cosmopolitan outlook and solidarity with people in need. We've taken in many of them without creating the social tension that is a well-known factor in other countries. But politically, we mainly represent ourselves. We make a distinction between positive and negative neutrality. We not only spread our values and interests offensively, but defend these values and interests too. The state and its institutions may do all in their power to maintain these positions, but if the people do not identify with them, nothing is achieved. We've discovered that a cosmopolitan population like ours naturally leans toward neutrality. How should people who come from all over and have such different opinions regarding so many things get along with each other otherwise?"

"You're describing the current state of many urban centers. But you call it a heterotopia."

"And why not? You may be able to recognize similarities here and there between our society and those of other countries. But overall, we challenge the apparently apodictic reality of the outside world. And that's not all: we go beyond the systemic status quo. The systemic status quo is based on a maxim that I believe to be hopeless: 'If you're not with me, you're against me.' According to this principle, the world is always divided into two camps, the one innovative and other reactionary. But I believe that the two camps often permeate each other and therefore don't exist in a purely contradictory state. Do you know what I suspect? Utopia is not a place, but a volatile condition that can appear anywhere and at various places at the same time. We've not leased innovation here. Foucault compared a heterotopia to a mirror. I'd even say it is a concave mirror. It focuses innovative, utopian forces that appear somewhere in our time. And it sends back the messages into the ether of this age. We don't always know who's receiving them, but we know that they're being received out there."

"Low wage earners and billionaires inhabit your heterotopia. How long will social inequality be accepted?"

"Forgive my optimism: I believe in reason. Not just that the citizens of this island are reasonable, but people in general. You see, construction workers or unskilled workers come here because they can find better living conditions than at home or elsewhere in the outside world. Billionaires settle here, although on the face of it they could get away scot-free with living more cheaply somewhere else. Why? Because they're reasonable. They understand that you cannot have everything, but with intelligence and a bit of good luck you can have enough. The people who wish to live and work here, Filipino housewives as well as French scientists, assume that their future here has more to offer than the one at home. They believe in this future, you see. They're optimists, just like me."

"Injustice remains injustice."

"If I understand you correctly, you consider inequality to be unjust. I admit that I don't share your opinion. The classic left-wing and right-wing positions have left people in an impasse. Some believe the world is unjust because it apparently treats people in an unequal manner, while the others believe the world is unjust because it apparently treats them equally. We should recognize that inequality is unavoidable within a certain framework. The social, cultural, biological differences don't allow any point of view where everybody can be viewed as equal. It's all about the framework. Inequality is growing to an outrageous degree in the outside world. We're trying to restrict it. Inequality becomes unjust if nothing is done to reduce it. Any society in its early stages, while growing, can fight injustice and yet respect inequality."

"Growth is the pride of your principality. But it's well known nowadays that growth is double-edged. It could come to an end tomorrow—also here on the island. How sustainable is your project in the long term?"

"It goes without saying that our development needs to be sustainable—in the sense of ecologically acceptable, socially just, and culturally prosperous. But I'd still not say that sustainability is the driving force behind our strategy. What does 'sustainable' really mean? A rust-proof electric vehicle? A vegan diet? A secure pension? The problem is that we're often uncertain what it means. Particularly if we're talking about a period of one generation or more. What you've just said about growth is true of sustainability: in many cases it may well be over tomorrow. I believe the issue of sustainability is developing into a bubble similar to the issue of mobility a few decades ago. In light of the overused airspace and road networks, the accident and sickness rates, the destruction of the environment—which goes hand in hand with our mobility—we can only draw the conclusion that the way mobility has been conceived since the Second World War has created huge problems. Mobility is a social bubble that's long since burst. It's also interesting to note that there's hardly been any appreciable progress in this field. Nothing's happened since the space-shuttle program. Whatever car and aircraft manufacturers sell as a revolution is no more than slightly more comfort and safety in an increasingly uncomfortable and unsafe world. Sustainability could create a new bubble. We produce goods and create services that will, for example, last longer and be more effective than their predecessors. But what if it turns out that we should no longer produce these goods and services or use them for reasons that we don't even know yet? Sustainability claims to have a knowledge of the future that we simply cannot yet have. We now believe that gold has a stable value. The Portuguese four hundred years ago thought pepper had a stable value. Are four hundred years sustainable? I'd say that the principle of sustainability assumes a static value system. But we need dynamic systems where sustainability is just one criterion among many."

"So what stimulates sustainability on the island …?"

"The ability to adapt, tolerance. Vigilance about the fleeting nature of our forecasts. The world has become so complex that we know less and less about it, even though we know more and more. Forecasts about the future are being corrected at shorter notice than ever. We constantly need to relearn what's happening and draw consequences immediately. Sustainability may be one of them, but that's it."

"Your society's a late arrival and is benefiting from globalization. Because others have exhausted themselves in modernist projects and optimizing capitalism, your time has come. What makes you so certain that you'll not be visited by the virus of exhaustion in the near future?"

"I'm not aware of any certainties. But we are observing the outside world. It's true that it is not particularly well prepared for globalization—in the West now less so than forty years ago. At that time, most people worked in industries, like vehicle manufacturing or chemicals, that were already globalized. Assembly-line workers in Detroit or the Rhine-Main region in Germany felt the effects of competition from the Far East as early as the 1980s. Then people migrated to the services sector and started to work as lawyers, teachers, and nurses. Those are all local professions, and not linked to globalization. So we have to prepare people better for globalization. We're doing that by developing our own society. That's certainly easier to do here and cannot be put into practice in America or China overnight. People there need to adopt different approaches."

"You're observing the situation in other countries. What's going wrong there?"

"Generally, countries are relying on technology. They maintain that it's the solution to many severe problems. I agree with this up to a certain point, but there are two restrictions. Firstly, technology tempts people to believe that they can manage the world, despite historical experience. Because history teaches us differently, technology is celebrated as novelty in itself. It's supposed to liberate us from the errors of the past. I believe the world is only partly manageable—it's partly unmanageable too. And it's very possible that precisely the unmanageable part of the world offers a solution. Secondly, I quite frankly cannot discern any raging technological progress. Yes, we have Silicon Valley and the IT sector. But is an iPhone really an achievement that can be compared to the Apollo space program? Or to the discovery of the controlled splitting of the atom, the light bulb, or the Otto engine? And what exactly do we expect from technological progress? It not only simplified our lives in the past, but also created jobs. I don't know of any industrial sector among the new technologies that is appreciably compensating for the gigantic loss of jobs that has been caused by the rationalization of classic industries."

"Steelworks and coal power will not experience a revival. What advice are your economists offering?"

"Let's assume for a start that many sectors don't experience a technological boom, but a downturn—sectors like heavy industry that require expertise that you can't develop overnight. We're keeping our hands off of these. But there's one player in the current economic situation that is often treated as a hindrance in the discussions about technological innovation—although it concerns the main productive power! I'm talking about the human being who deserves, as you would say, closer inspection in this discussion. It seems to me that the reason for marginalizing human development is that at first sight it promises little creation of value. Humans are 'expensive': this statement, from a moral point of view, does not reflect reality, but it's true from a material point of view. Even if we were computers, we'd have to recognize that the costliness of humans does not automatically speak against them as the main productive power. The island plays a role here. If our model was exclusively based on the principle of a regulated financial market with a free trade of goods, we'd be a tiny developing nation moving toward a perhaps unusual form of democracy. But we have more in mind. We generate huge revenues in order to invest in 'expensive' humans. Perhaps it's occurred to you that our Social Fund creates jobs ..."

"Didn't your economists warn you about the project of the Social Fund? It smells of that musty social market economy of 1970s Europe!"

"If you're trying to say that the market economy wasn't really musty, then I agree with you. But it's become unaffordable because the market and society can no longer live in harmony. The social market economy is an oxymoron in current circumstances. If we want to change this, we'll have to change both elements, the market and the society. That is precisely what we're working on. Our market model is a combination of the controlled financial sector and free trade. Our social system creates opportunities instead of supporting hopelessness."

"You need to explain that in more detail."

"OK ... then I'll tell you a riddle! A farmer leaves behind seventeen horses and a will after he dies. He assigns his inheritance to his three sons according to the following ratio: the first son receives half, the second a third, and the youngest a ninth of the horses. Now find the solution!"

"I assume this is a trick."

"Then you're doing the dead man an injustice. We both know that you can't divide seventeen horses into halves or thirds without causing a bloodbath. But look, in the countryside the people talk to each other about their problems. So the three brothers seek help from a neighbor. The neighbor finally has an idea. He lends the brothers one of his horses so that they now have eighteen. The ratio suddenly works perfectly: the oldest receives nine, the middle son, six, and the youngest, three of the animals. And to increase the miracle, the horse that the neighbor has lent them is left over."

"Back to the people on your island."

"I'm with them, Stascha. I fear lest the outside

world acts like you, and cannot solve the riddle. Instead of lending a horse, the inheritance is gradually being slaughtered. Woe if the transaction does not pay off! Well, the transaction is not particularly beneficial for the neighbor. He doesn't lose anything, and only gains little. So why does he help? Because he's a neighbor and in the countryside neighbors generally help each other. We may not be in the countryside, but with a great deal of economic expertise we're establishing an unprofitable economic zone. We're lending horses to people that have a project so that they can complete their project. If all goes well, we'll get our horse back. You're familiar with the unprofitable economic zone known as the Social Fund. The outside world has abandoned any faith in the need for these kinds of zones. But that's precisely our opportunity. The society that we have in mind is not more profitable, but simply more humane than others. We spend a lot of money on art and culture, on international aid projects, on young people who have amazing ideas, and we don't inquire about our profits. We make a quality of life that has now become unimaginable in your home country possible in a social world."

"And maintain capitalism ..."

"We don't want to copy or improve capitalism or even abolish it. We want to use it to liberate people from a few shortfalls. Do you realize that humans are deficient beings? You and I are deficient beings. But often a little effort is enough to help people eliminate this deficiency. This effort is the difference between a developing nation moving toward democracy and us. Do you know what we've discovered in making this effort? The main deficiency is that we're accustomed to exclusively judging situations in terms of profit and loss. It's true that human beings are egoistic. Whether you believe it or not, they're also selfless. Altruism is perhaps the most underestimated virtue. It's true that prosperous societies tend to foster envy and egoism. But people are not doomed to follow their tendencies. The island hosts a prosperous society. We still intend to rehabilitate the idea of altruism."

"So you're promising a better society. Aren't you afraid of being accused of misleading people?"

"These kinds of accusations don't bother me. I'm not promising anything. I'm just optimistic. Optimism is viewed as either a sign of stupidity or ideological deception. It's now easier for most of us to imagine the end of the world than a life of light and merriment. True, a dystopic view of the future has its magic. But it's a black magic. We're not involved in performing magic here. We're just tilling our field."

The man with the white hair and the almond-shaped eyes nods to Stascha. The monitor goes blank. An image appears on the screen: www.lavapolis.com.

The Most Popular Article

1. Politics
2. Immigration
3. Universal Solidarity
4. Economic Development
5. Autonomous Territories
6. Private Capital Investments
7. Social Fund
8. Education
9. Time
10. Gray House
11. Prediction Center
12. Universal Agora

Lavapolis, an island country in the Mediterranean Sea, has a landmass of 246 square kilometers and is located southeast of Sicily, west of Crete, and north of Libya. The island was settled by Theodore Messinis in 1946 after five hundred years of devastation caused by the now-inactive volcano Mount Buono. Faidon is the current prince of the island.

Politics

1982, the second year of Faidon's reign, saw the end of the autocratic hereditary monarchy, and universal suffrage with ballot voting was introduced. The adoption of a constitution paved the way for a constitutional form of government.

The citizens in the principality now elect a national council consisting of forty-eight members, which shares exertion of power with the prince. The constitution may envision an extensive right of assembly and freedom of speech and art, but it does not allow the formation of parties. Instead, political interests are catered for through the principle of a populist democracy.

This principle envisions that parliamentary candidates run for office with individual political programs. They normally reflect the area of political work where the candidate has already obtained officially recognized expertise. While informal arrangements between candidates on individual bills are permissible, they may not organize joint election campaigns or create formal, permanent alliances.

The principle of populist democracy emerged out of a deep sense of skepticism about multiparty democracies that dominate European politics. The collapse of the party landscape in neighboring countries like Italy, Greece, and France in particular destroyed any faith in these kinds of institutions as the legitimate and efficient tools of democratic representation among most of the islanders.

The short history of the island, however, has produced a form of populism that should not be confused with manipulative political movements whose short-term success often depends on charismatic individuals and a rhetoric that oversimplifies reality. The wave of counter-democracy currently sweeping across Europe and America has emerged among grassroots movements on the basis of intense resistance against established politics. It is fed by an insatiable rage of negativity toward everything. On the island it is viewed as an irreversible crisis in the party culture and therefore as a confirmation of the alternative course adopted by the principality more than thirty years ago.

Despite the differences and historic distance, our practice of populist democracy tends to recall the spirit of the People's Party in the United States one hundred years ago. In contrast to the goals of established parties, this party represented the interests of the simple people, particularly in rural regions. The movement had a major influence on the political culture of the United States for a while. It was the People's Party, for example, that helped implement restrictions on office terms and voting by secret ballot.

Populist democracy, as practiced in our principality, is partly based on a self-regulating mechanism and partly on a departure from vested interests by the members of parliament. The division of power between the patron and the legislative body, which has been anchored in the constitution, demands a stronger, direct role on the part of the citizens than is normally the case in representative democracies. This involvement is enabled by the assessment system in the <u>Universal Agora</u>.

The government is formed on the principle of concordance. The eleven members of parliament with the highest shares of the votes become members of the cabinet and the post of prime minister rotates every six months.

The island has only just over five hundred thousand residents as well as a relatively small territory and generates a correspondent GDP. As evidenced, this provides good conditions for the rapid introduction of a populist democracy. Although there was repeated political unrest during the first two legislative periods, when the patron had to make use of his right of veto and once even disbanded the national council, our system has now proved reliable, even in crisis situations. The members of parliament are now elected for four years and have to run for office with an individual program each time. According to surveys, a high voter turnout is achieved because the candidates' diverse programs reflect the content and guiding principles of every political inclination covered by the principles of the constitution.

Immigration

Populist democracy has proved to be a vehicle that can cope with the high speed of population growth. Today six times as many people live on the island than when Faidon assumed power: in 2014, the figure was 617,000. The demographics of our country speak for themselves: 37 percent of the residents have local citizenship; eighty-three nationalities are represented in the principality, including every European country as well as the larger nations around the world; the island is home to large numbers of people of every different faith; around 170 different languages are spoken; the average age is thirty-one.

We make use of the principle of stimulated and controlled immigration. People applying to reside in the principality are subjected to a health test and an interview that is designed to give the jury information about the candidate's professional and cultural skills. This also applies if local companies are recruiting people, unless the public administration body itself is involved. Any placement by labor agencies is only acceptable in the case of minimum-wage recipients. These agencies are subject to regular checks to ensure that they exercise proper care toward employees.

The relatively high proportion of citizens can be traced back to the fact that individuals can be naturalized after a period of five years of residence, regardless of their country of origin. They go through a naturalization procedure that also includes a test of their loyalty to their new home. Citizens are allowed to hold several passports.

This rule has created a situation where nationality of choice has grown by several tens of thousands, or at least 5 percent, every year. The interest in becoming an islander is huge among immigrants. Our immigration policy aims to make electoral citizens the majority of the population during the coming decade.

Those without the right to vote still enjoy the political right of participation. All the relevant decision submissions are initially introduced and discussed at virtual public hearings before they reach the parliament. These hearings take place in the Universal Agora and people can follow and comment on them via videopod. Supporters and opponents of these submissions not only present their arguments, but also face questions and opinions in a public forum, which each official resident on the island can access. An assessment tool caters for the right of participation, because various policy options are evaluated in advance in the Universal Agora, similar to the well-known user ratings on the Internet.

This principle represents one element of populist democracy that is the result of the nature of our intense immigration practice. It implies a pragmatic use of participation, very much like a populist democracy itself. Our experience has shown that people welcome the right to have a say and rarely abuse it. The population has a fundamental trust in our municipal authorities and the government. People only participate if an issue specifically interests them. Unlike traditional democracies, the expression of political opinions is a tool for solving problems, not a weapon of constructive mistrust in the system itself.

Conditions of immigration exist for those seeking political asylum. There are about four hundred refugees in the Hermes reception camp, which the island operates without any outside support. Their cases are carefully checked according to the internationally binding measures of human trafficking and counter-terrorism, and our authorities are able to come to a decision in only a few weeks. Around two-thirds of these asylum seekers can find jobs in the local employment market. The others are sent back to their countries or handed over to the care of relief organizations that operate on the island and whose charity projects are supported by the principality's Social Fund.

Illegal immigration and human smuggling have been largely eradicated. Thanks to the program passed jointly with neighboring Mediterranean countries a few years ago to protect maritime borders, a closely knit control system of drones and land robots has been installed on the North African mainland and off the coast. We have emerged as winners in the technical battle between the smugglers and the authorities. Attempts to escape are almost invariably halted on the territory of those countries, from which numerous, often unseaworthy boats had set off for the north in the past. Their passengers often became the casualties of those irresponsible operations.

The principality supports the North African nations not only in the battle against illegal migration, but also in handling its causes and consequences in the sociopolitical arena. The island supports medical and hygiene campaigns in the relocation camps in these countries. Primarily, the Autonomous Territories Cooperation is helping to improve the general economic situation in various countries on the continent.

Universal Solidarity

Our Charter of Fundamental Rights has much in common with the United Nations declaration. The right of each individual to achieve his or her own happiness was taken from the US Constitution. But the Charter of Fundamental Rights differs from these laws in one point: anchored within it is the right to universal solidarity. The special feature of this right is that it enjoys priority over the right to other types of solidarity like religion, the nation, class, or sex. You can summarize this principle as follows: what joins people—regardless of where they come from or whichever deity they believe in—is more important and enjoys a higher standing in law than what distinguishes them.

(Many countries state that they act according to this principle. But this is not normally the case. Let us take the right to freedom of religion. The problem exists in the conflict between a certain faith and the legal and ethical consequences that arise in practicing this religion. For example, Islam is recognized, but any Sharia jurisdiction allowing polygamy or physical punishment is banned.)

Our charter does not claim any absolute universality of values or identities. Following the principle of "What joins us comes before what divides us," we aim to achieve a feeling of solidarity among our citizens that is strong enough to form a new identity. This identity functions on the basis of belonging to the principality's society. Loyal islanders view themselves first and foremost as citizens of this island, regardless of whether they are originally from China or the Netherlands. Relocation from the outside world to the island does not simply correspond to a move from one country to another. We tend to view our citizens automatically as world citizens. Those who settle here no longer represent a country, but a network of all countries, cultures, and religions.

The creation of a universal identity and solidarity is one of the most important goals of our social policy and one of the greatest challenges for our citizens. Many people who move from the island to a foreign country have difficulties breaking loose from their former solidarity.

We do not attempt to form a classic national identity. This is normally the result of a cultural affiliation transmitted by history for the majority of the population and their current interaction with themselves, the outside world, and the minorities in their own country.

Our country cannot draw on any historical tradition or any significant definition of majorities and minorities. The only alternative is to have the cultural affiliation of the majority as well as each minority on the island as the basis of our identity.

As the citizens are from nearly all the countries on Earth as well as widely differing social milieus and religious denominations, *the Charter of Fundamental Rights only grants them the right to maintain their faith or their national identity, etc., if this does not conflict with the overriding right of all the people to universal solidarity,* the most important fundamental right on the island. Social or moral distinctions are exclusively respected within the framework if these distinctions in turn respect the universal *conditio humana.*

The core of our identity is therefore nonnational, nonreligious, and nonclassist. Legal practice excludes the possibility of anything that contradicts universal solidarity.

We view this rule as the offer of a new homeland, not as an exclusion process. In fact, we expect our new citizens within a particular transitional period to integrate into a society in which the status of a citizen on this island has a higher standing in the law than the color of one's skin, their religious affiliation, or their national background.

Our social policy reinforces integration and weakens differences. Those who intend to settle in the principality have a claim to assistance measures from the solidarity program. This program backs ecumenical and inter-religious marriages, for example. It influences the school system, which exclusively evaluates pupils according to their technical and social skills and does not recognize any social privileges. As our education program is structured in a universal manner, global players on the education market, like "international schools," do not receive a license here.

The profile of our policy is internationalist and secular. Women make up 45 percent of the seats in the parliament and government. Public and private media are required to pursue balanced intercultural reporting.

The solidarity program does not reflect a dominant national culture or a melting pot. Identity on the island, according to the directives, represents variety.

The universal language of art can help each citizen to transfer his or her personal national identity into global citizenship. Our artists are therefore encouraged to help shape a narrative that fosters solidarity through the history and society on our island. *Each citizen acts as an artist on his or her journey to this new identity.*

Everybody is invited to participate in setting up the Universal Agora, which was founded in the Gray House two years ago in 2014.

Economic Development

Thirty-four billion euros have flowed into our country during the past five years alone. In the same period, 26 billion euros were invested in economic, social, cultural, and research projects on the island or in the <u>Autonomous Territories</u>. The relation between deposits and GDP is at a favorable level of 1:1, below average for industrial nations. The financial resources based on the island are used to generate wealth to a greater degree than in many parts of the world. The principality is one of the most competitive countries.

Current economic policy rejects any offshore practices and offers a system of comparatively low taxes too. This island is not a tax haven or a state bureaucracy. The financial concept adopted on the island responds to the increasingly precarious dilemma between inefficient tax regulations and contestable avoidance practices. This policy is based on moderate but reliable long-term growth—in contrast to other developed economies. In addition to the traditional sectors of tourism, construction, logistics, and financial services, development projects, particularly in the <u>Autonomous Territories</u>, have played a major role.

The economic boom directly emerged from the social development of the island and its history. Seventy years ago Patron Theodore was confronted by difficulties that would have certainly intimidated any lesser politician and forced them to throw in the towel. Most immigrants were fishermen and farmers. Skilled workers from the cities would only arrive if there were prospects of employment in modern production sectors.

Using the income from the territories leased to the US armed forces as well as a number of development loans, Prince Theodore ensured that the necessary infrastructure was set up to stimulate tourism. Permission for gambling then followed. Barring a few corruption cases—which he cracked down on—the economy took off. By 1960 the island was enjoying the reputation of being equally desirable as a holiday destination because of its tourist services and its natural beauty. An upswing, unparalleled in the whole region, had begun.

Prince Theodore has been accused of selling off the island and subjecting it to a type of economic monoculture. It is true that at the end of the Theodore era it looked as if the island was at the mercy of the casino-trap. But by today's standards, Messinis thought and acted globally from the outset. The import of American pop culture was the driving motor that raised the island from its political and economic nonexistence. This gift of being able to think big at the decisive moment is one of the most important traits that his son inherited from him. Faidon's mission was to cast off the monoculture of casino capitalism and reshape the island into a hub reaching out beyond the immediate region.

This mission required a diplomatic offensive in every direction. Both father and son had adequate experience of blackmail and bribe attempts by foreign governments and foreign companies. When the accusations from the Arab region became too great on account of the American presence, Faidon used this argument to restrict the presence of the US Navy at Cape Dolphin, north of Mount Bouno and the southern territorial waters. Relations with the Council of Europe and Arab League gradually normalized. The island joined the United Nations in 1997.

The diversification of the economy, the renunciation of the casino-island image, and the buildup of the island into an international hub by expanding Bouno Airport and constructing Container City should be viewed in the same light: they reflect this global mission. While other cities in the Mediterranean region had to struggle with corruption, civil wars, minority conflicts, and a reluctance to introduce economic reforms, since the 1990s the island has been able to remain the only functioning trading area between Western Europe and the Emirate States in the Persian Gulf. When logistics giant Maersk, Cathay Airlines, and Nestle opened their first large-scale branches in 1999, financial journalists still had to study the map in order to discover exactly where Lavapolis was.

A short while later, many of the internationally important service providers set up business on the island. The principality became a base for developing building and agricultural resources in the sub-Saharan region. The Autonomous Territories project now guarantees constant growth for our economy.

Autonomous Territories

The cost of imports from Europe and the food prices on global markets rose alarmingly at the end of the 1980s. Lacking any appreciable agricultural space, the Faidon administration contacted various governments in central and eastern Africa. It took several years to establish stable relations. Our first investment was in northern Nigeria; this was followed by large groundbreaking agricultural lease agreements in Madagascar and in the south of Sudan.

At the beginning of the Autonomous Territories Cooperation—

named as such after the project was successfully launched—lease agreements were signed with the relevant African governments. The island exclusively operated on government property for a long time and only after ten years of experience in the region did it negotiate with the local authorities to cultivate land in village communities.

This original restriction turned out to be a blessing. African tribal ownership is clearly divided into many small plots of land that belong to individual families. Everybody knows the border marks of their unit, but the land has never been mapped. In order to lease tribal property, all the units had to be surveyed. Our government only started mapping territory after it was possible to use GPS. (Many international rivals did not carry out any surveying work and later clashed with the farmers because neither side could prove how much land was actually involved in the lease arrangement.)

At the outset, the island exclusively signed short-term contracts. The legal situation was usually confusing and colonial laws had not been systematically reformed. Foreign investors normally boost corruption as a by-product of this legal inheritance. Our government has had better experience with regulations that take into account the interests of the farmers too.

By 2000 the island had leased a few thousand hectares. Food Care, our agency for international agricultural management within the Autonomous Territories Cooperation, now cultivates five and a half million hectares of agricultural land in Madagascar, Ethiopia, and Sudan—and in Sierra Leone since the end of the civil war. According to official information, this corresponds to roughly one sixth of the land leased this way worldwide. Food Care produces rice, rubber, oil, coffee, and various kinds of fruit. More than forty thousand people work on our plantations. Most of the raw materials are processed in the country and sold in the continent.

Once our agricultural activities had successfully started, we expanded our operations to include economic development and social projects. Of course, this was only possible in countries that are fairly stable politically. Food Care grants long-terms loans with low repayment premiums.

More recently, investments have been made in the construction of infrastructure. Many Food Care investors are citizens of our island. Given the volatile global economy, they have been convinced that it pays to invest capital in Africa in the long term. The nations in which we operate the Autonomous Territories Cooperation are today some of the fastest growing economies in the world.

A national economy of our magnitude depends on networks to be able to reliably survive in overseas projects. Food Care normally cooperates with a number of partners from other industrial sectors. For example, we have supplied sixty thousand homes with power by working with a solar-cell manufacturer in eastern and central Africa.

Networks of this kind require a strong cooperative instinct from their actors. Food Care has primarily succeeded in setting up a portfolio in Africa where our commitment to agriculture flourishes alongside our commitment to infrastructure and the social sphere. Several investment projects are only economically successful within a larger context. Indirect profitability is viewed as a strategic goal for many economic initiatives on the island. For example, the electrification campaign: electricity means a higher standard of living, a higher standard of living supports social and political stability and higher general productivity, and this benefits agricultural yields in the end.

The government views with skepticism how Western industrial nations and developing countries in Asia and the Arab Gulf region are occupying huge areas of African countries with their own resources and exploiting them for their national interests. Of course, countries like China or Saudi Arabia must make arrangements in order to cope with both the rapidly growing need for food and their local climate, which is unsuitable for agricultural production. But the leased lands are usually operated as economically extraterritorial zones. The local economies hardly benefit from the yields. On the contrary—thousands of farmers are often robbed of their source of income after corrupt governments have signed dubious lease agreements with international food corporations without showing any interest in those who cultivated the land in the past.

Even the term "Autonomous Territories" indicates that our society is not interested in the practice of land grabbing and does not view the leased lands as the island's economic exclave. Since 2000, this project has enabled us to attach several billion US dollars in long-term investments to African countries that help them establish a healthy economy.

Private Capital Investments

The incentive offered by our island and its small national economy to private foreign capital is a financial consequence of the long-standing global indifference toward Keynesian warnings of unfettered monetary capitalism. The law of private capital investments establishes a new kind of connection between the physical presence of an immigrant and the location of their assets.

It is possible to purchase citizenship on the island for a certain period by making a contribution of five hundred thousand euros. The funds accrued through this commercial naturalization process flow into the Social Fund, a state agency, which is responsible for creating jobs and social security insurance, among other things. The time restriction on naturalization does not apply if immigrants spend at least six months of each year on the island over the next five years. They are entitled to import capital to an unlimited degree when arriving and pay a one-off tax of 10 percent. In addition, they can use their new citizenship to shed the old one.

(Critics say that we grant illegal asylum to financial refugees. However, passport shopping is rather popular in the outside world. Each year the United States grants paid residence to ten thousand applicants. And we should recall that even some EU nations still either allow the short-term purchase of citizenship or the unrestricted and untaxed import of capital, or even both. In Great Britain, for example, the purchase of "non-domiciled residence" is only a minor administrative hurdle for citizens of many nations. Certification allows them to import assets and purchase property without having to pay taxes in return. Belgium enables the straightforward transfer of citizenship within a few years for EU citizens. Furthermore, a growing number of people live in several European nations at the same time because of job migration, and it's becoming increasingly difficult to allocate them to one national tax authority. People with large assets and employees of international corporations and organizations can barely be assigned to one territorial nationality anyway because of their multiple places of residence and employment.)

There is currently a growing and complex conflict between national identity, internationally distributed assets, and migration for governments and individuals alike. We are defusing this conflict by ensuring that any capital from immigrants who have paid for their citizenship is not just coupled to a tax payment, even if it is relatively low, but also an obligation to invest. Those who want to become citizens of this island through purchasing a passport automatically opt to invest at least one third of their imported capital in the country in the course of the twelve months following naturalization. Future capital imports must be registered with and legitimized by the tax authorities. If they are not subject to outside tax obligations, a similar rule applies to capital that was originally imported: one third of the imported sum must be used in the territory of the principality.

The Capital Investment Act is attractive simply because of positive economic development. A high degree of competitiveness promotes the constant growth of imports of assets.

At the same time, the requirements for non-domiciled owners of capital have been adapted to match the current security and legal standards in the international arena. Our laws do not protect money laundering and tax evasion here. We still insist on data secrecy as long as there is no reasonable suspicion of any criminal activities. This is based on the progressive legislation enshrined in our constitution.

Social Fund

If the Autonomous Territories represent a geographical expansion of our economic activities, the national Social Fund could be labeled the "autonomous territory" of the island's market economy.

The Social Fund combines three functions that are performed by independent agencies:

Firstly, the Social Fund seeks to stimulate employment. In this sense, it is comparable to the national job agencies in the outside world's social market economies. But while these institutions have had to migrate toward safeguarding the social basics for workers who are no longer able to participate in the production cycle because of the decline in economic power, our agency for employment has a growing jobs market, which causes us to continually recruit workers from the outside world.

Secondly, the Agency for Infrastructure and Technology promotes new industrial and research fields.

The thirdly, and perhaps most unusual, function of the Social Fund is the result of the Agency for Promoting Unprofitable Production Sectors. A society only forms a healthy organism if it maintains types of employment that do not hold out any prospect of long-term success in the free market, but that are valuable for the development of the *conditio humana*. These include the fields of education, health, politics, and culture. They are becoming more and more important globally, but the material resources for maintaining them in the public arena are becoming increasingly scarce.

The global crisis in the public sector is clearly evident in the huge bottom-up redistribution of capital and assets. The principle of localizing imports of capital (private capital investments) on the principality's territory is a partial attempt to prevent this development. As a result, a considerable share of the tax income is fed into the Social Fund in order to support unprofitable production sectors—from the time they are set up, if required. The income generated from the sale of citizenship is also used in the Social Fund to support unprofitable areas of society.

The Agency for Promoting Unprofitable Production Sectors currently has 1.4 billion US dollars at its disposal. This is the equivalent of almost 5 percent of the GDP. This high degree of expenditure results from the fact that, on the one hand, members of socially weaker classes are given education opportunities and free basic health care and, on the other,

innovation is supported and stimulated.

While most private investments worldwide are absorbed by innovation projects in technology, social and cultural value creation and improvements are dramatically undervalued. This issue is especially critical because not only is the consumption of culture rising, but a completely new form of the production of cultural goods and services is being created as well, which is not just a result of, for example, technological advances in the field of media communications. On the contrary, a combination of technological hardware and expertise on the one hand and huge growth in the need for cultural articulation on the other have led to an explosive distribution of new cultural materials and products—through open-source portals, for instance. More and more people are involved in the public arena and in art. Artistry is viewed less as an artistic mission and more as a social one.

Over the last twenty years, many countries have equipped their young people with excellent skills, only leaving them to wallow in poverty. The Social Fund in our principality offers these young people an opportunity that they no longer have in their home countries. The Faidon administration does not, however, intend to create unrestricted professional institutions for the practice of cultural activities. The sad current reality in Western countries is that institutionalizing culture, apart from a few exceptions, is no longer viable.

The Agency for Promoting Unprofitable Production Sectors registers applicants with different qualifications and offers them the chance of participating in real production processes. It recognizes, for example, the younger generation's special expertise in developing new types of social communication both in the real and the virtual public arenas.

The island likes to see itself as an expanding public entity, but its shape is not determined by the state. The agency entitles third-party organizations or individuals to develop the public arena. For this purpose, it uses cultural workers who otherwise have little opportunity to use their knowledge because of the market situation in the outside world. The agency provides resources and defines objectives and timetables with the contracted groups. The use of these cultural workers in the field of social housing, for example, ranges from designing flats to organizing programs at public squares. They are not paid with money in each case, but with

benefits to cover their rent, further training, or health insurance. The agency's budget therefore contains a nonmonetary part, which supports the aim of jointly locating social and financial capital on the island. Although it is responsible for unprofitable production sectors, the agency generates a high degree of indirect profitability. This is not just measured in terms of economic data, but in social and aesthetic benefits too.

Education

Last year, in 2015, the school system was expanded to include a voluntary program of Interactive Home Schooling in order to encourage the transfer of knowledge and experience across generations.

Rapid technological change, primarily in the field of communications and data processing, has ensured that both the inventors and the users of these technologies are becoming younger and younger. Ever since a seventeen year old sold a smartphone app to Yahoo for thirty million US dollars, teenagers have become the norm among software specialists. Market analyses show that the average age of users of new IT products has fallen by six years over the last decade.

As a result, the market is increasingly geared toward the

interests of the youngest generation of consumers. This development is not in any way restricted to data processing. The influence of minors on general consumer behavior has increased drastically. As purchasing power generally declines, this group forms the only growing consumer clientele in the outside world. The influence that this generation has on the production of forward-looking technologies and their markets is therefore just as momentous.

While experts are closely watching and making use of the role of teenagers in the creation of market trends, the effects on the social relationships between generations, and particularly between children and parents, have long been underestimated. The last thirty years prove that succeeding generations not only develop different sociocultural behavior to a previously unknown degree because of their conditions of learning and maturation. Critical educational theory now assumes that a *fundamentally* new attitude toward knowledge and technology is developing among young people. Adolescents, for example, view social competence completely differently than their parents.

Young people adapt to social and communicative changes in their environment faster and more efficiently, which accelerates the erosion of parental authority. The invasion of innovative technology in everyday life has already radically transformed social relationships within families. It is clear that children and teenagers develop a greater ability to absorb new technologies that have become indispensable for everyday life. But the marketing of new technology is always associated with the spread of new ideas and content. (Design changes not only technology, but behavior as well.)

The result is interactive software for coping with life, developed by IT specialists as they communicate with their many millions of underage followers, and no longer compatible with parents' social understanding. This process of developing social software bestows privileges on those who participate and excludes those who do not. The moral concepts and everyday worlds of young people and parents are drifting apart at a vehement pace.

If this trend continues to accelerate, we can assume that future generations will consist less and less of age groups.

While modern technology creates an advantage for young users compared to their parents in regard to application and knowledge, which go far beyond this technology, young people are reaching sexual maturity years later than before the turn of the millennium, due to the deterioration of nutrition in many countries.

Although this last issue does not especially apply to the overwhelming majority of young people living on the island, our education experts have drawn attention to the risk of forming parallel worlds that alienate children and parents from each other.

Interactive Home Schooling is a program developed for families living on the island to counter this trend and strengthen the integrating forces between the generations.

The project is based on two observations:

Firstly, the enormous transformation of everyday life has already led to a significant incoherence in young people's personality development. We are observing a preference for technology-related values over social values. Technological innovations have reached a degree where children can overcome time and space restrictions beyond their wildest dreams. The associated experiences of speed and algorithmic actions dominate the formation of social traits. People experience the world as an object that is technically "manageable" and therefore artificial. In contrast, their experience of the real world is increasingly restricted to basic life issues like biological needs or unavoidable routines (school, weekends, holidays, etc.). Their above-average degree of maturity in coping with the artificial world contrasts with a below-average degree of maturity in handling the real world.

Secondly, these developments have created a morally defensive position in many adults. They feel excluded from the culture of innovation or feel provoked by it. Busy with the tasks of the real world, they view the new daily opportunities offered by the artificial world as an unreasonable challenge that causes them to constantly regain their bearings and adapt to ever-changing technology and knowledge. Adults tend to avoid modernization, while teenagers show great enthusiasm for it.

Clearly, mirror-symmetric tendencies to the real and artificial realities of today's world have now effectively developed in both generations. These tendencies often trigger irreconcilable conflicts.

Interactive Home Schooling attempts to bring the two generations closer with educational courses where the roles of teacher and pupil are not fixed, but vary depending on degrees of competence.

The family becomes a forum where there are no set authority levels. The relevant knowledge issues are formulated as problems and the parents/children collective has to solve them together. Depending on their knowledge, the members of the collective act as either teacher or pupil.

Interactive Home Schooling fundamentally distinguishes between two thematic groups. The first group deals with the hermeneutic acquisition of information technology. Making use of familiar procedures from game theory, intellectual techniques are imparted that, for example, explain the mechanism of operating technologies in new user programs. A knowledge of applications is augmented by a knowledge of how applications function. Teens often take on the role of teacher in this topic, and parents, the role of pupils.

The second topic deals with a hermeneutic acquisition of social competence. Parents and children often swap roles here. Values deserve their name today only if they provide orientation in an environment of permanent interaction, changing prospects, and anonymous players. Absolute values have proven impracticable, because they are irrelevant in this environment. Any general relativism in values would in turn serve the trend of forming parallel worlds, as described above.

The topic dedicated to acquiring social competence is therefore devoted to ideas on how cultural and moral values enable some consensus that can be accepted beyond generations and social classes.

Interactive Home Schooling presents the problems in a form that makes it impossible for people simply to retreat into conventional behavior. An adult in the role of teacher does not stand on the solid ground of unshakeable moral facts from which they can spread their wisdom to the next generation. Interactive Home Schooling includes the anarchistic adage of "Everything is permitted." The task of the collective of teachers/pupils is to negotiate a high degree of consensus between possible moral values. To achieve this, the program offers procedures for this thematic group. With their help it is possible to acquire life experience that would be foreign otherwise, and a platform can be created from an isolated standpoint. Game theory offers guidance here on how to test and adapt these kinds of procedures within a family collective.

More than fifteen thousand families tested Interactive Home Schooling during its first year.

Because it is a voluntary program, this result encourages us to assert that the family continues to be the nucleus of society.

Time

In the 1950s, as the settlement of the island was beginning, the media theorist Marshall McLuhan recognized that progress through electronic communication technologies largely consisted of overcoming spatial distances and collecting the world at one place. McLuhan introduced what later became the legendary term "global village."

What McLuhan had meant to be positive turned into pessimistic criticism twenty years later: the monitor screen annihilates space. While real space had detached objects from each other, electronic media were concentrating objects in a non-place. Live broadcasts on screen were proof that the traditional human space/time concept was being obliterated and the broadcast places themselves were being destroyed.

The Faidon/Martel research paper from 1984 may well support these opinions, but it concludes that it makes sense in the long term to break the synchronization between local time and the world clock. This suggestion was introduced at the end of 1996, the year Europe standardized its rules for summer time. Since then, the island has set its own time.

News broadcasts to and from the island now take place with a delay of one minute. (Anybody who derides this asynchronicity as an absurd notion underestimates the effects that an autonomous time system have in an almost completely networked world. Financial real-time transactions are therefore impractical. Unrestricted flows of capital, which are beyond time and space and elude any kind of control, are now viewed as the main disease affecting the global economy in the outside world, but they are brought to a halt at the time border of our island and become manageable again.)

Gray House

The prince's residence, where the Prediction Center and the Universal Agora are located.

Prediction Center

A statistical authority with an executive function: the most important state body within the Department of Strategic Planning. Logging and analyzing data help to provide tactical control mechanisms. Using selected methods of probability and game theory, forecasts are made about the development of the principality.

The center employs a large number of analysts who follow economic, social, and cultural procedures using real-time tracking, and evaluate big data. They depend on the participation of many of our citizens. Systematic surveys and measurements enable them to know, for example, how many people are using public transportation, how the population feels about transit tourists, or the use of local food products.

Universal Agora

a.   An assessment system to guarantee political involvement. All residents on the island have the right to become actively involved in the political decision-making processes via their videopods. Official proposals are presented in the Universal Agora and citizens evaluate and qualify them. Thanks to this form of collective voting, the populist democracy has a strong self-regulating factor.

b.   A virtual collection of objects, biographies, anecdotes, and documents with which the citizens of the island and people across the globe enrich the great narrative about the evolution of our society. It reconstructs each event that has taken place on the territory of the island or each thought that has gone through the mind of a resident, if the persons involved permit recordings and agree to their documentation in the data-protected archives in the Agora.

www.lavapolis.com

Note on Sources
This book is based on experiences, observations, and reflections I have made during the last years while working and living in places particularly exposed to globalization. Written sources that were significant for obtaining information and insight were: Nicholas Shaxson, *Schatzinseln* (Rotpunktverlag, 2011), Jörg Dünne and Stephan Günzel, eds., *Raumtheorie* (Suhrkamp, 2006), *ARCH+*, no. 208 (2012); and *Spontaneous Interventions: Design Actions for the Common Good* (www.spontaneousinterventions.org).

Acknowledgments
I am grateful to the people—family, friends, and colleagues—who sustained me throughout the work on this book.

BIOGRAPHY

Michael Schindhelm, *1960 in Eisenach, former East Germany, studied quantum chemistry in Voronezh in the former Soviet Union, held positions of opera and theater director in Berlin and Basel, and has worked as writer, filmmaker, and cultural adviser in Dubai, Beijing, Mongolia, Moscow, Hong Kong, and various European countries. He lives in Lugano (Switzerland) and London. www.michaelschindhelm.com

COLOPHON

Solution 262: Lavapolis is part of the Solution series
edited by Ingo Niermann and designed by Zak Group.

ISBN 978-3-95679-070-6

Series editor: Ingo Niermann
Book editor: Max Bach
Translator: David Strauss
Proofreader: Niamh Dunphy

Design: Zak Group

Printed and bound by BUD Potsdam

This book is accompanied by the transmedia storytelling
project "Friday in Venice."
www.lavapolis.com/fridayinvenice

Sternberg Press
Caroline Schneider
Karl-Marx-Allee 78
D-10243 Berlin
www.sternberg-press.com